o ...tion to build understanding of real issues fires her own writing.

Kissed to Death is Gillian's second novel set in Portsmouth, where she grew up in the aftermath of World War Two. It follows *Bombweed*, the successful adaptation of her mother's wartime fiction.

With love to
Peter
Gill
x x

KISSED TO DEATH

GILLIAN FERNANDEZ MORTON

SilverWood

Published in 2021 by SilverWood Books

SilverWood Books Ltd
14 Small Street, Bristol, BS1 1DE, United Kingdom
www.silverwoodbooks.co.uk

ISBN 978-1-80042-079-3 (paperback)
ISBN 978-1-80042-080-9 (ebook)

British Library Cataloguing in Publication Data
A CIP catalogue record for this book is
available from the British Library

Page design and typesetting by SilverWood Books

*To my mother, for pointing me towards writing
and to Irene Caspari for showing how
important children's stories can be*

Also by Gillian Fernandez Morton

"Reading Bombweed took me back to my childhood, the love, fears, partings, the families living through war and its repercussions... This is a beautifully written book. The reader is drawn into the time and place, seeing, hearing through description and dialogue, and feeling the emotions of the characters so well portrayed. I was there from beginning to end and reluctantly read the final page. Women are often ignored in stories of war. Bombweed helps to fill that gap."

– writer of prize winning poetry and short stories,
Margaret Campbell

The snow-flakes grew larger and larger, till at last they looked just like great white fowls. Suddenly they flew on one side; the large sledge stopped, and the person who drove rose up. It was a lady; her cloak and cap were of snow. She was tall and of slender figure, and of a dazzling whiteness. It was the Snow Queen.

"We have travelled fast," said she; "but it is freezingly cold. Come under my bearskin." And she put him in the sledge beside her, wrapped the fur round him, and he felt as though he were sinking in a snow-wreath.

"Are you still cold?" asked she; and then she kissed his forehead. Ah! it was colder than ice; it penetrated to his very heart, which was already almost a frozen lump; it seemed to him as if he were about to die – but a moment more and it was quite congenial to him, and he did not remark the cold that was around him… The Snow Queen kissed Kay once more, and then he forgot little Gerda, grandmother, and all whom he had left at his home.

"Now you will have no more kisses," said she, "or else I should kiss you to death!"

Hans Christian Andersen,
The Snow Queen

"No evil dooms us hopelessly except the evil we love, and desire to continue in, and make no effort to escape from."

George Eliot,
Daniel Deronda

Prologue

London
1944

Even now, when she shuts her eyes, she sees him.

It was the smell of him that had come first, even before she heard him emerging from behind that tree in the dark of the blackout. Beer, cigarettes and something else, something sour and animal-like. A smell which, after it was over, clung to her.

Yvonne had been walking across Southsea Common on her way home after the evening shift in the King's Arms. She'd liked the space after an evening of noise and crowds in the bar. These days the blackout never bothered her. The faint light from her torch was enough to see her feet. It was July so it wasn't cold, but the wind was suddenly quite strong.

No one was around to hear her cry out. Then she was sure he'd have hurt her more if she'd shouted out again, once he'd got her arms tight from behind and was wrenching her dress up, forcing her legs apart, shoving her face against the tree. The taste, the feel of eating bark. The sharpness of his knees against the back of her thighs.

A feeling of being ripped open, and the horror when he'd gone. She could hear his boots stumbling, running across the grass, leaving behind his smell. If she gets a waft of smells like that in the pub, or on the Underground of an evening, she has to stop herself from retching. Even now.

Somehow, she'd got home, got herself up the narrow stairs, trying to stifle the sobbing so Mum wouldn't hear. *Mum mustn't know.* First to the bathroom, dragging her damp flannel from its hook, scrabbling to turn on the tap to wet it, desperate to get clean, washing and washing, again and again, then to crawl into bed with her flannel between her thighs, horrified at the sight of the blood, and turned to put out the light. Trying not to cry with the pain, she'd called out to Mum to say she'd eaten something bad – didn't want anything – 'No, nothing, thank you!' Would she ever want to eat anything again? Or look at herself in a mirror?

When she missed her periods, Yvonne had wanted to get rid of it, hated to feel the alien presence of something growing, something left inside her by force. It wasn't long before Mum realised what was up. They'd argued and argued about getting rid of it, giving it away, but her mother was adamant that it wasn't the baby's fault. Any baby deserved love. And she could help Yvonne bring the poor little thing up, couldn't she? Her mum said they'd tell people Yvonne's secret "fiancé" had gone down with his ship in the Pacific. There were a lot of stories like that in wartime and people could think what they liked. But however many times Mum said "baby", Yvonne could only think of an "it".

After the boy's birth – again, a feeling of being ripped open – Yvonne had tried, she really had, but seeing it looking up at her, she knew it'd be seeing a piece of trash, a dirty piece of... like she saw if she ever looked in the mirror. She knew she'd have to go away. Felt bad about taking the money from Mum's old jam jar on the mantelpiece, but she'd needed it for the train fare to London. Easy to lose yourself up there, people told her, to get some kind of a job in a bar or a club. And so it was all right, in a way, apart from the disgusting smell of beer and sweat from the men that made the bile rise up. And, of course, the dreadful raids, interrupting conversations or dreams. Mind you, she did find herself drifting off sometimes when it wasn't too busy. Would find herself back on the seafront. Before the war started and all the barbed wire blocked it off. Watching the waves with Mum in the old shelter, smelling the seaweed, hearing the seabirds squealing and quarrelling. Sitting out of the wind and staring at the boats on their way to the Isle of Wight. Her mother was always saying how one day they'd go on one of those big ferries for a treat. Have ice creams on Ryde Pier and even a donkey ride. But it never quite happened. Now, up in London, the Second Front was all people talked about. And of course, the doodlebugs. People often said, carelessly, 'if it's got your number', but you could see the fear that still flickered for a moment over some part of their face.

Back in her tiny London bedsit, Yvonne is carefully scraping out the last of her lipstick with an orange stick, then spitting onto the remaining scrap of mascara, getting herself ready for the evening shift at the pub. When she hears the approaching roar of a doodlebug, she thinks, everyone says you are OK if you can hear it but when the noise cuts out— In the sudden

11

silence Yvonne catches a glimpse of her own terrified face in the mottled mirror, a second before the house fragments around her.

Part One

Crane Street, Southsea

1948

Elizabeth Siddons, hanging out the washing in the back yard, hears the plop of the soggy tennis ball on the wall of her terraced house. It's a comforting sound, reassuring her that her Gemma is playing outside with Kenny, the little chap from across the road who lives with his granny. They're still only four, but she's sure the children are safe enough out there. Hardly any cars. It's a dead end. Only ever the postman wobbling up on his bike, or the milk cart. How has that old tennis ball survived the drooling jaws of the street's dog? He appears as if by magic whenever the children are there, hitting the ball back and forth against the bricks.

The boy's not at the age yet to be asking questions. His granny has told Elizabeth how it worries her at night. Sarah says she'll explain when Kenny's old enough to understand. Not yet though. He won't have any memory of his mother, she says.

Elizabeth would like to ask more about Yvonne's pregnancy but has never pushed. Growing up so close in this street the children are like brother and sister. At least Gemma's got a dad, even if she's seen precious little of him. Donald's still in uniform, away in Europe, dealing with the chaos in Hamburg's ruins. She guesses he'll turn up before long to get his demob suit for civvy street. Elizabeth isn't sure if that's something to look forward to or not. And he'll be like a complete stranger to Gemma.

Elizabeth realises she's been so caught up in her own thoughts that she's stopped pegging out the sheets. She reaches for the next damp, heavy whiteness to lift, spread and clip to the line. As the slight breeze lifts a few strands of hair off her face, she looks up, her attention drawn to the small biplane slowly making its way across the blue sky towards the sea. A good drying day, she thinks. Nothing to worry about now, but she's never lost the habit of listening out for a plane's engines, feeling a tiny sense of relief when it's gone on its way. Silly really, now the war's well over, but she knows she's not the only one. Those years here in Southsea left their mark on most people. After the Phoney War there was the shock at those first raids and then all the getting used to new things like the siren (Moaning Minnie everyone called it) that could turn your legs to jelly – running for the nearest shelter if you were out in a daylight raid – then the anxious hours waiting for the "raiders passed" signal. Nights huddled in the Anderson shelter, wondering what you'd find when you emerged, which house collapsed, which neighbour caught, either out in the street or under a falling wall or roof. People disappeared in so many ways. Everyone said they got used to it. 'If it's got your number on it…' they'd say, before complaining about the lack of soap or butter.

Elizabeth bends down to separate two red woollen socks embracing in her basket, and stretching back up, pegs them next to the last sheet before putting a hand to her spine, rubbing the stiffness as her thoughts drift. When someone just didn't come back...from abroad or just from the shops...or going off like Sarah's daughter, Yvonne, so soon after she'd had baby Kenny. All too hard to get one's head around. Someone you knew well enough to store a picture of them in your head, someone maybe you'd been impatient with the last time you'd seen them...and then nothing. Sometimes you'd see the telegram boy on his way to a door. Sometimes literally nothing. Like old Mrs Mortimer, the doctor's wife from the next street. Caught in a raid on her way home from the WVS. Nothing much left to put in the coffin, but no one said that out loud in front of the family. But her poor daughters...

Stepping back, Elizabeth checks her full washing line with relief. Hearing the tennis ball again, she wonders if the children will be off to the bombsite down the street where they often go when they aren't bat-and-balling on the outside wall. She's often watched them running in and out of the ruin's tall pink weeds, hiding from each other behind the half-walls as they play their endless games of make-believe. Sometimes children from the next street show up, all different shapes and sizes. Noise and sometimes tears, scraped knees, torn jumpers, and fallings-out. Nothing a bit of broken biscuit and a glass of lemonade in her kitchen won't put right. A wonderful playground now, but it had been someone's home. Still signs of it there, but broken and unoccupied, rosebay willowherb and buddleia half disguising the damage. Elizabeth shudders inwardly, for a moment picturing the young mother who didn't get to the shelter in time. Sarah thinks that when everyone else in the street heard the siren, poor hard-pressed, slightly deaf Hilda, must have been rushing to get dinner done before her kids got home from school. Probably with the Home Service on loud, so didn't hear the warning. Hilda's sad children live up north now with grandparents. Elizabeth is glad Gemma and Kenny won't be dwelling on the implications of the rain-stained scraps of floral wallpaper, which cling to one standing brick wall. But some things are hard to forget.

Elizabeth, with a small exhale of breath, pops the remaining pegs into their drawstring bag and, taking the handle of the empty basket, turns back towards the house.

Sarah Crawley, hearing the thwack of the bat on the tennis ball and the children's laughter, looks from her upstairs window across the road and smiles as she repins her grey, untidy bun by feel. No use for mirrors at her age, and how many times has she put her hair up in her fifty-eight years? She loves to see them out there and as long as they are back in someone's kitchen by teatime doesn't fret.

It's Monday. Elizabeth will be hanging out the washing. She's a good friend. Brings her hot soup when she gets a bad cold, came in every day when she had that fall and couldn't even totter down to the Co-op. Sarah thinks it is time to cook Gemma's mum a fruit cake, she's been saving up a few currants for it. Elizabeth loves her cake. Sarah loves Elizabeth's smile. But she's uncomfortable when Elizabeth asks about poor Yvonne. Sarah's only told her the bare bones or, rather, the official version of what happened to her daughter. But this thought is a reminder. She needs to decide what to do – will have to explain it to Kenny in some way one day. Doesn't want to tell fibs but how can she possibly tell a little boy that kind of truth?

*

In the street, Kenny is brushing a dark fringe back from his damp forehead with one hand as he stands watching, resting his bat, as Gemma tries to reach the tennis ball before the dog gets his teeth around it. Gemma battles with the dog. 'Oh no, you don't, Champ. Give it here,' she says, and when she's retrieved the ball after a tussle, throws it back to Kenny, laughing and wiping her salivary hands on her shorts. He takes his best swipe to send it flying back to the red bricks. Gemma makes contact with her old tennis racket and sends it off again to hit the wall, but Kenny misses the shot and has to chase it down. With the soggy ball in one hand and his bat in the other, he stops to catch his breath for a second and hears the creak of his upstairs window over the road. Kenny watches his granny as she looks out and up at the sky. Momentarily he catches her frown, her downturned mouth, but then she's smiling down at them both, patting her coiled hair in that familiar way.

'Milk and biscuits in ten minutes, if anyone's interested,' she calls.

Kenny knows he was born in February 1944 because that's what Granny Sarah has told him. Of course, he doesn't remember that. No one remembers being born. Anyway, now he can recognise the big numbers on his birthday cards. Granny has shown him photographs, just one or two, of him when he was little. One is of him being held, wearing a little knitted bonnet, in a group of grown-ups outside the church in the next street. He doesn't recognise the grown-ups, except for Granny Sarah and Mrs Siddons, Gemma's mum, both smiling at the camera in smart hats and coats. The lady standing between them in the photograph isn't smiling. She looks as if she's seen something strange and worrying on the other side of the street. The other picture is of him lying in a big box, like a drawer maybe. He isn't smiling either. He has a thumb in his mouth.

Now, at four, he is allowed out (as long as he stays in their street) so he and Gemma, who is a bit taller than him even though two months younger, play ball on the wall of Gemma's house, or best of all, go down to the bombsite at the far end of the street. He and Gemma love its broken-brick corners, dark and smelly with mould, which lurk beneath tall, pink wild flowers. Places to hide, places to pretend you are a robber or a cop, Robin Hood or the Sheriff of Nottingham, or with the help of an old hat or some pigeon feathers, a cowboy or an Indian.

Kenny thinks there must be something secret about this place. Nobody talks about it, but he and Gemma spend many hours there. If he ever feels an unpleasant question rising in his head, he gets rid of it, hits it away with his bat, chases it off as he tussles with Champ. Life is too busy for questions.

Gemma doesn't recognise the man who walks up the path. He's limping a bit and is in a uniform. Elizabeth has told Gemma that her daddy is coming home. She can't remember who this is, even though her mum has told her that Daddy has met her once, but she was too young to remember. Gemma doesn't quite follow what Mum says, but it is something about far away serving his country and, since the war ended, helping people to get things straight after all the problems there.

It seems like her mum is pleased, and she has put on her special dress with a big rose pattern all over it, which she normally keeps for best, and her long fair hair looks all shiny. This makes her smell different from usual, not unpleasantly so, but it is unsettling. This man puts his arms around Elizabeth and then bends down to put a hand on Gemma's curls. The hand feels heavy and rather rough as it lands on her head.

At supper they sit round the kitchen table, three of them, instead of the usual two, so Gemma's chair is in a different position and she has lost her usual view of the room, which feels odd and a little disturbing. They eat a stew and some greens and a bowl of Gemma's favourite pudding, which she and Mum call fluffo, because of all the bubbles. It is made of evaporated milk and red, wobbly jelly cubes, which you have to tear apart (she loves that bit), before pouring on hot water so they can dissolve. Then it all has to be frothed up by the whisk. Elizabeth sometimes lets Gemma do a bit of the whisking. She likes the noise it makes when she turns the handle really fast and watches the tiny bubbles appear. You have to leave it then in the cool larder to set. It can be hard to wait.

Tonight's meal is either awkwardly silent, or the two grown-ups start to speak at the same time and then both laugh. Gemma just listens. The man is drinking something brown with a bit of froth on top from a glass. He has a moustache, and Gemma is fascinated by the tiny bit of froth that is clinging to his hairy upper lip. When Gemma gets up to go and get ready for bed, the man bends again to kiss her on the cheek and the smell of him is a bit sour. She thinks it is from what he was drinking. She feels uncertain. He looks like the man in the framed photograph on the sideboard who is called "your daddy". Except in some way she can't connect him to it.

Kenny's friend is usually in shorts and Aertex shirt, with grubby knees and tangles of fair curls. One day he and Granny are invited to a special tea at Mrs Siddons' house. Today, when Gemma answers the door, she looks all different in a floral frock with smocking across the front and a small white collar. Her hair is brushed almost straight and there is a gigantic, shiny pink bow pulling her hair off her face to one side. In the living room a large man sits in a chair near the window. He is in uniform. His thick, scratchy-looking jacket is brownish with lots of badges and pockets. Kenny scans the room for clues and notices the hat on a chair, sitting there like a snoozing cat. He is still staring at it when he hears Mrs Siddons say, 'Kenny, come over and say hello to Mr Siddons. This is Gemma's daddy.'

The man gets up and comes towards him, holding out a big hand. After a second or two staring at the hand, wondering about the thin white scar snaking its way through dark hairs, Kenny realises he is expected to touch it. When he tentatively moves his fingers towards the hand, the silence seems to go on forever, and then suddenly everyone is talking at once so Kenny can sink into the background. He doesn't think he has ever touched a man before. This is new. Hasn't ever seen Gemma in a frock before either, or with a hair ribbon. He feels a grumble in his head and a tightening in his belly. He moves back and takes Granny Sarah's hand, turns himself towards her to blot out the scene and hides his face in her skirt, which, comforting-ly, always smells a bit of their little kitchen. Listening hard for clues, he hears that Mr Siddons is back from somewhere where there has been fighting. Kenny has heard about the war but doesn't understand. He's caught scraps of conversation between Granny and Gemma's mum, but they always stop when he comes into the room or the garden, or wherever they are talk-ing. He isn't sure if that's because it isn't anything important, or it's something too dreadful for him to know about. Listening now, from behind Granny's skirt, he worries that his best friend has disappeared and been replaced by a stranger. Has Gemma gone forever? He feels an emptiness now in his head. And then a new feeling. He thinks he hates this man.

A few days later, Gemma knocks at his door, wearing her usual old shorts and shirt, her untidy curls no longer grasped by a hair ribbon.

'Hello, Kenny, it's only me. Don't look so surprised. Come on, it's not raining.'

They are soon off down the road with the tennis ball, and the old bats. 'My daddy's gone away again,' says Gemma, 'but look, Kenny, he bought me some sweets from the tuck shop before he went off. He said he'd have got more if they weren't still on the ration. Let's go down to our camp and eat them, like a picnic.'

Kenny feels as if the sun has come out.

Sarah Crawley never sleeps well these days. At night, wide awake, tossing from one side to the other, her thinking goes round in circles. She wonders why she'd persuaded Yvonne to keep the baby. It had seemed the right thing to do, and anyway, she had so wanted to have lots of babies herself after meeting Cyril. On the pier it was, in 1914, and oh, didn't they catch each other's eyes, with the sound of the waves on the shingle and the chinking of the slot machines and the sun beating down? The wind had caught her hat and he'd run after it. And when he came running back with it and smiled, they were just standing there, the two of them, just looking at each other for a long moment, before they both started speaking at once. And then they were laughing – he had such a lovely smile. Cyril had proposed one day, only weeks later, while they were sitting in the old shelter along the seafront watching the waves. He said he was sure, and hoped she was too, although people would say it was so quick, he knew that. But anyway, he wanted to be engaged now, as in no time at all he was off to the Front. After their marriage, when he was on leave that Christmas, they'd hoped to start a baby, but it didn't happen then, nor on the other brief chances of being together. When Cyril came back eventually, he'd been in no state. She had been longing for him – had hardly seen him for the four years of the Great War, and when he was back, after the gassing and everything, and all those nightmares, when either he couldn't bear anyone near him at night, or he'd be clinging to her, sobbing into her chest like a baby. Well, making babies wasn't very likely, so when little Yvonne came along in 1924, after her years of wishing and him occasionally trying, it had been like a blessing. A miracle even. She was glad that Cyril was able to see the baby, but he lasted only another year before his lungs gave up. At least she had the small pension from his time in the army. So how could she say no to another baby in the house? Even if Yvonne could only talk about an "it". Turning and tossing, listening for the milkman in the early hours, she thinks that maybe if she'd let her daughter go away to one of those homes for young unmarried mothers, she'd have been back and might even be here now, or married to some decent local chap with a good job. And maybe with several babies for Sarah to cuddle.

She knows she will have to tell Kenny something about all this history one day. She has even kept Cyril to herself, although why? Perhaps because if she once got started on talking about the past, it would somehow all come out. Sarah keeps thinking she'll do it when he is older. But really, it is because she can't bear it. She remembers all too well the shock, like a punch in the stomach, of hearing poor Yvonne vomiting in her room next door early one morning. And the next, and then the next. Then Sarah knew all too well what kind of sickness it was. And coming after weeks of her normally chatty girl's silence and the way Yvonne's staring eyes seemed to be looking at something not quite there. It took a while to get the story out of her. The attack in the blackout, late at night, as Yvonne was walking back across the common after her shift. (Hadn't Sarah told her often enough to stick to the main road on her way home? But she wouldn't listen.) Neighbours had talked about her – at her age, working in a pub – but she'd been a good girl, only trying to help her mum with the housekeeping.

Yvonne had cried that day when they first talked, and they'd wondered for a while what to do. No point in reporting it. Who would believe a slip of a girl who thought it was OK to work in a pub at night, serving all those men in uniform? They both knew what people would say. When the baby inside her was beginning to show itself, and after a lot of arguments and tears, Sarah had insisted. They had put together a story of a secret engagement to a sailor, (George, they'd decided to call him), who'd gone down with his ship in the Pacific. 'Yvonne and George had been planning to marry on his next leave,' they would say, if people asked. And sometimes, even if they hadn't asked, but had momentarily flicked their eyes down from Yvonne's pale face to her growing waistline. People either sounded sympathetic or cynical.

Yvonne cried again when Kenny was born, after being in awful pain during the long, frightening labour in the little up-stairs room. Then she'd cried again in distress, as the little boy gazed up at her from the old dresser drawer, which Sarah had organised for his first bed. Sarah had hoped it would just take time. And then one morning, she had got up to find that Yvonne wasn't there. Her ration book was though, and her other identity papers, sitting on the kitchen table next to the scribbled note on the back of an envelope, saying not to worry about her and that she just couldn't do it.

Hamilton Road Infant School
1949

It is slightly before nine o'clock on a chilly morning in early September. Elizabeth and Sarah stand with the children by the gates of the nearby infant school, each child clutching a grown-up hand. The tall, grey-haired woman who emerges from behind an imposing wood-and-glass door, lifts and lowers a heavy bell by its leather strap purposefully. The sudden metallic sound startles some of the more nervous five-year-olds. The woman holds the bell in one hand while she unlocks the gate and gestures for the children to enter, raising a stern hand at one mother who tries to follow her son into the school. As hands are reluctantly released, eyes glance anxiously backwards and forwards, hearts beat a little faster and the gaggle of new children go through the gate for the first time. As they disappear behind the door, rather like the children in the Pied Piper story, thinks Elizabeth, the knot of women are left with hankies to faces, arms holding onto neighbours' arms, tearful smiles shared, before feet turn towards home. Some maybe head to a shared cup of Camp coffee and a gossip, others perhaps slowly return to an empty kitchen to have a good cry. But not for long, as the laundry will still need to be done.

Inside the school hall, the children are sorted into two classes. Kenny and Gemma find they are in the same one and turn to hug each other. Shown into a room smelling of polish and disinfectant, they try to sit next to each other, but are frowningly pointed in opposite directions by the tall, grey-haired woman.

'Boys that side near the windows, girls this side nearer the door. Quickly now.'

When he has found his seat, Kenny glances across to the other side hoping to catch Gemma's eye, but she is staring ahead at the marks on a big blackboard. He has never felt so alone. He is still staring into space, bewildered, when he realises that the woman sitting at a big desk in the front is looking expectantly at him, and he blushes when the boy behind nudges him.

'Just say "Yes, Miss Batchelor".' When he does this, the woman's attention moves on to call out another child's name. This is a different woman from the bell-ringing one and she is young and pretty, Kenny thinks, with dark, curled hair and a pink-and-white face. And this one smiles. By the end of the morning, Kenny has learned that he must listen for his name and reply when Miss Batchelor calls it out from the register, and that he mustn't otherwise speak unless the class is asked a question, and, even then, only if he has put his hand up first and been chosen. Halfway through the morning he is desperate to do a wee but isn't sure what to do. What if he can't keep it in? When the bell rings for playtime he rushes to find the boys' urinal and just makes it in time, before looking all round for Gemma. At first, he can't see her and whirls round and round, searching the corners of the yard, looking for her familiar face, in a panic, until he feels her tap on his shoulder.

By the end of the first week he feels a bit more comfortable, but hates the questions he can't answer. Sometimes it's because he hasn't been listening. Has been staring at some of the pictures on the classroom walls. There's a really interesting one of a place he has been told is called Egypt, with camels in front of huge and strange-shaped buildings. But sometimes he has just been staring out of the window for no reason. Miss Batchelor often tells him to stop daydreaming. Gemma usually gets the right answer and seems to know what the chalk marks on the board mean. He wants to know, and Gemma says she's going to help him.

Kenny has found some old friends in the other class, Harry and Leslie, who he has played with on the bombsite, and that's a relief. And on the first Friday afternoon he is excited at getting a large, clean, empty book for drawing. He has always liked drawing. Granny Sarah keeps a pile of old, rough wallpaper scraps for him, and he has been given crayons and pencils for birthdays and Christmases. Today he likes the feeling of this new sharp pencil sliding over the page as he tries to draw his house – until his drawing goes all wrong. When he turns over a page to start again, he is told off for wasting paper. He is glad that it is Friday, he tells Gemma on their way home. The next day, they play cops and robbers together on the bombsite as if nothing has changed. But somehow, Kenny knows deep down that it has. On Monday morning he feels a bit sick and wishes he could stay home.

Suddenly it's September again, and somehow a year has gone by. Kenny can understand the marks on the board and in his reading book, and he can draw a really good picture of a house now. But a page full of sums gives him the heebie-jeebies. He and Gemma are sitting on the crumbling stone wall in the bombsite, following the butterflies with their eyes. It is the day before the new term starts, before the first day in a new class. The usual weeds growing high around them are losing their summer purples and yellows. Gemma is blowing on a white dandelion clock. Kenny has told her that someone at school said you could tell the time if you counted how many puffs it takes to get rid of the white fluff. Four puffs means it's four o'clock. He doesn't tell Gemma that another boy said that if you pick dandelions, you'll wet the bed. Kenny tells himself that's nonsense. But feels uncomfortable in case it is true. He still remembers the shame of his cold, wet pyjama bottoms, not even that long ago, when, for a while, he couldn't wake up in time. Granny had always said kind things and helped him into dry bottoms after changing his sheets, but he had worried because her face looked cross in spite of her words.

Gemma is looking forward to the next day and school again, she says, and wonders what the new teacher will be like. Kenny is sorry the summer is over, but doesn't say so. He hopes Granny Sarah won't want to walk him to school. He hates it when he hears the other kids say things about her and how old she looks. He wants to walk up the road with Gemma, but he knows she'll probably run off if she sees one of the girls she knows – the ones she usually plays with at lunchtime. They do skipping songs and dancing games or squeeze up together on a bench, whispering. He has boys he plays with, but none of them are special – except Harry and Leslie, the ones from the next street who have always been around, and still sometimes join in the games on the bombsite.

After the first week in her new class, Gemma is glad to be back. The teacher has given out nice clean exercise books to everyone, with a space to draw and a lined area to write on every page. Miss Newey also starts each morning, once the register is done, by reading a Bible story to the class. And some days she takes them into the hall and puts on a wireless and Miss Newey is quiet and they listen to the lady with a posh voice on the wireless telling them to move around the room without bumping into each other, and stop and start, and be a tree and now curl up like a little mouse, and things like that. And when some music plays, Gemma loves to move in time with it. When she looks across to see how Kenny is doing, he looks either a bit anxious or is giggling and grinning with another boy. Miss Newey sometimes asks him sit out on the bench for five minutes if he does this too much. Actually, Kenny loves to hear the music and his body wants to move with it, but when it happened the first time the other boys laughed at him, so now he messes about. He'd rather be told to sit out than be laughed at by the other children.

Gemma looks forward to playtimes and runs out when the bell rings to find her new group of friends. Someone always has a skipping rope and she's learned some new games. She likes the feel of the rope swinging over and back when it's her turn to hold one end, and she's getting better and better at the jumping too, loves feeling the way the moving rope just misses her feet each time. She often catches sight of Kenny scowling across at them from the other side of the yard, even though he seems busy kicking a football with his friends, and anyway, he says, skipping is sissy and just for girls even though he and Gemma had often taken it in turns with her old rope in the bombsite or the back garden, seeing who could count the most unbroken jumps.

When Kenny and his friends come and chase them with roaring faces and waving arms like mad soldiers, the girls all shriek and run to another corner of the playground, and Gemma isn't sure if they are really scared or are just pretending.

At midday Kenny likes to run up the street beside her when they go home for lunch. But she has heard other boys teasing him, and saying, 'She's your girlfriend, she's your girlfriend!' It annoys her. His embarrassed frown tells her he hates it too but doesn't know what to say back. After things like this, Kenny may run ahead of her or dawdle behind when they go back to school for the afternoon. One day she heard some of the boys calling out things like, 'Your gran looks like a witch,' and 'Ain't you got no mum and dad?' When she told Elizabeth about it, her mum didn't really answer, except to say how unkind boys could be.

It gets dark so early now, Kenny thinks, as he tries to make his Christmas lantern just like the teacher has shown the class. There is still a small glow from the fireplace that's been keeping them warm each day since the weather got cold. It is a Friday afternoon in December and, like every Friday afternoon, they are doing craft. All the class are making the same kind of Christmas lantern today. Glancing round, he sees that Gemma and the children on her table have nearly finished theirs. He's managed the first bit, folding the thick rectangle of black paper in half and cutting slits from the fold nearly to the other edge, and he has bent the sides round to make the lantern shape so the slits open up. Now he picks up the glue brush again and tries to place the small pieces of coloured tissue paper over the slits, but it is hard to get the glue in the right place and he feels all fingers and thumbs. He likes the slightly sweet smell of the glue paste but hates the feel of it when it gets on his fingers. He senses the teacher approaching, but doesn't mind as she is kind as well as pretty, and speaks quietly.

'Having a bit of a fight with that glue, Kenny?' she says. 'Let me give you a hand. I'll hold the lantern out flat so you can stick on the coloured paper. And then we can bend it round to join the sides. You'll see. It will look like the light is shining through the gaps when it's finished.'

'Thank you, miss,' Kenny says gratefully. Miss Newey smells of something nice when she is near him like this.

It is his second year at school and he has made some progress. He is on harder reading books, like Gemma. He doesn't mind that she is a bit further on than him with the stories about a boy and a girl and a dog. Sometimes he forgets and thinks the stories are about them, except this boy and girl have a mother with a big bright kitchen and a father with a suit and a car and a pipe. And their house is big and they have a proper garden. He always enjoys it when it is his turn to sit reading his book to Miss Newey, but sometimes he feels a flicker of something uncomfortable that he can't name as he turns the pages.

His favourite thing is still drawing. Miss Newey tells him she likes his pictures. He can write something under each one now, and it means he can make stories come alive on the page. He always looks forward to her reading out his words when he has finished, as if they make sense to her.

'Time to get your lanterns finished, children, and then clear up before we have our home-time prayer. Write your name on your lantern and put it on my table at the front. Don't worry if it isn't finished. We can see to that next week before we put our Christmas decorations up for the party. Gemma dear, will you collect the glue brushes? And Tommy the scissors. Careful, Tommy, to hold them safely the way I showed you.'

Soon the class are all standing, eyes shut, murmuring the home-time prayer. Kenny isn't really concentrating. He is looking forward to getting out of school and joining Gemma in the playground. It will be too dark to go the bombsite, but they can still play bat and ball in Gemma's back garden by the light from the kitchen window. This makes him remember Miss Newey talking about the light shining from his lantern. He thinks his next picture will be of a house in the dark with light shining out of the windows.

The July sky is grey, but on this day near the end of the summer term, it feels too warm for everyone to be all dressed up for the fancy-dress parade. This happens every summer now. Starting in the school playground, the procession will go winding all around the local streets, past the corner shop, past the park with the bandstand and the caged birds, past the pub, past the newspaper shop, before finishing back in the playground for the prize-giving. Anyone who has bought an entrance ticket can join in and the money goes to something called charity. Granny Sarah has said that means the money is collected for poor children who are sick or hungry. Gemma and Kenny are excited. A grown-up has come and pinned paper numbers on the front of them, and they have been shown where to stand in a line with the other children of their age. They can hear the sound of the small band that will lead the parade around the streets, so they know everything is about to start.

The children stand and stare at each other as they wait for the parade to begin. Kenny has a stretchy, stripy belt round his head holding the collection of dyed chicken feathers donated by his next-door neighbour, and he's got a toy bow and quiver of arrows, which he'd got from Mrs Siddons last Christmas,

34

over one shoulder. His last year's vest has been stained with tea by Granny Sarah, and he's wearing his old pair of shorts and sandals. Gemma's mother has painted his face with some of her lady's make-up. When he looked at himself in the mirror, he had a shock to see a stranger's face peering back at him with red streaks down each cheek and black round each eye socket.

Gemma is going as a scarecrow in her mother's raincoat, which reaches her feet, even with the belt tightly gathering it up at the waist. Mrs Siddons has threaded a stick through both sleeves so that they stand out each side, and tied bunches of straw to each place where a hand would usually go. Gemma feels peculiar and rather hot with her arms inside the coat by her sides. Mrs Crawley had produced a man's hat from the bottom of her wardrobe, and it is pulled down over Gemma's curls, and she's had something dark and smudgy put all over her face, done with a burned piece of cork. She's being tickled by the extra bits of straw that her mother has pushed round the collar of the raincoat.

As the parade starts to move off towards the school gate, there's a crowd of men standing on stepladders, with huge cameras from the local newspaper, clicking away. Gemma and Kenny are looking around in amazement as they walk slowly behind a group of much bigger children from the junior school. Everyone is staring around them, wide-eyed at the costumes and trying to recognise people, disguised and all painted or masked to look like animals, sailors, pirates and even cavemen. Maureen Smith from the next street has had some of her long red hair cut and has stuck some of it on her chin like a red beard. Kenny says to Gemma that it would be awful if Maureen couldn't ever get the beard to come off. Someone else has a big cardboard box around them, painted like a house with doors and windows, and a group of three bigger children are, one behind the other, inside a long cardboard box painted bright green to look like a train, with a puff of pretend smoke made out of cotton wool, coming out of a cardboard black painted funnel at the front.

'Kenny, you look like a proper Red Indian chief,' Gemma says, as they stride along.

The parade is picking up its pace, now it is out of the gate, and beginning to fill the street.

'And you make a really fine scarecrow,' Kenny grins back at her. But he is trying not to think about the hat. A man's hat. In Granny's wardrobe. It is a disturbing thought, but he can't quite frame the question it raises. But something doesn't fit and it reminds him of the boys who have sometimes chanted, 'Ain't you got no dad?'

What feels like hours later, the parade is back in its place in the playground. Kenny's feet are sore. His sandals are a bit small and have been rubbing his heels raw. Gemma is too hot, trussed up in the raincoat, her neck irritated by the straw bits, and her hands longing to escape into the fresh air. They spot Gemma's mum and Kenny's granny at the side of the playground waving at them. Kenny waves back at them, but Gemma can't, with her arms inside the old raincoat, so she wobbles her head at them and grins.

A man on a raised platform at the front with a megaphone is shouting out to everyone to make sure they are in the correct lines for their age group, because the prizes are going to be announced. There's a gradual hushing and stilling of the crowd. Smaller children are standing on tiptoes. Some of the smallest are scurrying about, helped by parents and teachers to get into the right lines. Then a fat bald man in a striped suit, looking important, wearing a big chain round his neck, starts to speak, but his voice sounds so crackly it's hard to know what he is saying. There's some clapping from the grown-ups and then numbers are called out to say who has a prize. Gemma jumps up and down when she hears that she has won third prize in her age group, but Kenny is disappointed, which makes Gemma feel awkward. The prize is National Savings Stamps in a little booklet and she tries to think how she can share these with Kenny.

Back in Gemma's kitchen there's a lot of laughing as Elizabeth and Sarah do their best to clean the sooty marks from Gemma's face and the make-up from Kenny's before they all sit down for a drink of lemonade and cake, one of Sarah's best sponge cakes with red jam in the middle, which she's brought round in her usual green tin. When Kenny and Gemma go out to the back garden, the two women fall quiet for a moment.

Elizabeth looks down at her fingers in her lap before asking, 'Sarah dear, Kenny's growing all the time. He must wonder… Gemma says that some of the boys say things…'

'I know, but…I try and start sometimes, practice the words in my head…but then don't get any further. He's still so little.'

'Sarah, love, you'll have to say something soon. What must he make of it? And anyway, is it so bad? I mean knowing that his dad died in the war? Didn't you say George drowned just before he was born? You could say his dad was a brave hero, or something like that, couldn't you? I expect his name will be on the big memorial on the common. You could take him to see it.'

Sarah is looking down, as if counting her fingers to see if they are all still there. When she eventually looks up at her friend's puzzled face, she says, 'Yes, yes, I know I could, Elizabeth. He's learned a bit about the war at school and from his mates. Knows that not everyone came back.'

'Oh, dear. It is difficult. For me too, in a way. But at least Gemma did get to see Donald, even if it wasn't for long. She doesn't ask any more when he's coming home. I've just said he lives somewhere else now, and it's too far away because of his work.'

Sarah nods, then looks away, blinking for a second. 'But at least Gemma's got you. It'll be harder to tell Kenny his mum just disappeared.' Her eyes water. 'Yvonne might still be alive, but what would that mean to the boy? That his own mother hadn't bothered to stay in touch? I imagine sometimes, you know, that one day she might walk back in through the kitchen door. But yes, of course. I know what you're saying and I'll try and explain more. When he's a bit older. I will, I promise. It's just that...well...'

'All right, Sarah, but don't leave it too long.' Elizabeth is looking up at the kitchen window, listening to the laughter and shrieks from the children outside. 'It's been a good day for them, hasn't it? With the parade and all the dressing-up.' She smiles at Sarah for a moment, but a new thought crosses her face. 'What about that hat? How long has that been there? You don't suppose Kenny might think it was his dad's?'

'It was Cyril's of course. He bought it when he came out of the army, when he got back from hospital in 1919. Once he'd convalesced for a while longer, he started looking for work, but he wasn't up to it, after the gas... Wasn't up to much at all for years... A miracle that Yvonne came along, given all that.'

Sarah attempts a bit of a smile and looks up at Elizabeth. 'But at least he lasted long enough to set eyes on his daughter...'

Elizabeth reaches out to put a hand on Sarah's arm as they hear the back door open and the children rush back in to ask if there is another slice of cake.

'One small slice each and then bath and bed,' says Elizabeth. 'But well done both of you. They must be exhausted after that great long walk, Sarah, don't you think? And didn't they look good?'

Sarah smiles at the children and starts to gather up her things. 'I'm leaving the rest of the cake for you, Elizabeth,' she says as she heads for the door. Then turning back, she catches Elizabeth's eyes for a second. 'And thank you for listening.'

Later Elizabeth is alone in the kitchen. Hearing Gemma splashing upstairs in her bath, she looks troubled. Getting up to stand at the sink, she starts to rinse the plates and mugs. Elizabeth remembers Yvonne, the slight young girl at the church for Kenny's christening, how the girl was given her baby son to hold by Sarah at the font, but who never smiled and soon passed him back. At the time, Elizabeth had put it down to wartime grief, as Yvonne's fiancé had gone down with his ship before Kenny was born. Now she wonders if she's not had the full story from Sarah. What makes it so hard for her friend to give Kenny some simple answers to the questions that must be arising in his scruffy, lovely head?

'Granny, the hat!'

'Pardon, Kenny love?'

'The hat that you gave Gemma for the parade. Where did you get it?'

'Oh, that old thing. It was down at the bottom of my wardrobe. Been there for years. I'd forgotten I'd still got it. Why, Kenny?' Sarah inspects her fingernails. Turns the old wedding ring round her finger a few times. Goodness this has got loose over the years. Poor, dear Cyril.

'But Granny, how did it get there? Who did it belong to?'

Sarah thinks, Elizabeth is right. He has got questions. But how to answer in a way that won't give him a shock? Too soon. Not yet. When he's older.

'It belonged to a man called Cyril, who I knew a long time ago. He was a nice man, a very kind man.' Sarah is looking out of the kitchen window now at Kenny's shorts and vest from yesterday's costume, swinging on the line next to the white sheets. She realises she's holding her breath, waiting for the next question.

'Granny, where is Cyril now?'

Sarah brings her gaze back from the garden where she has just pictured her Cyril, young and energetic, laughing, hanging out the sheets for her in the first few weeks of their marriage. 'He died, I'm afraid, Kenny. He was poorly, after being badly hurt in the Great War.' Sarah thinks, what else can I tell him now without upsetting him?

'Was Cyril my dad, Granny?'

Sarah freezes for a moment. Tries to speak in a normal voice. Wishes she had told him some sensible story from the beginning. And Lord, here he is now, seven years old. And she's not even shown him the photograph of her and Cyril on their wedding day. Him in his uniform all ready to go off to war. She could have put the framed picture out on the dresser like normal people, but she'd kept it to herself upstairs on top of the wardrobe. Kept it to herself like so much else.

'No lovey. Not your dad. He was your mother's dad. That means he was your grandpa. but he died...like your dad did.'

'Oh.' Kenny feels other questions pressing behind his eyes, but he knows he can't ask them now. Granny is looking so sad.

Part Two

Nothing Stays the Same

Years go by. No news of Yvonne. Elizabeth wonders when Sarah will give up hope. Elizabeth hardly thinks of Gemma's father now. Yes, Donald *did* come back, demobbed from the army eventually, after that cleaning-up stint in ruined Germany, but he wasn't around for long. He took a job as a commercial traveller selling brushes and dusters and tins of lavender-scented polish. 'Lucky to get the job,' he'd said, but it meant lots of days and nights away, and then after one trip he just didn't return. To be truthful, it was rather a relief. Although she keeps the framed photo of their wedding day on the sideboard, he'd never seemed the same man – the one she'd loved and married in such a rush in 1939 when war started. She thinks that his time in Hamburg, with all that chaos after the fire-bombing, had affected him even more than the fighting. She'd tried to get him to talk to her about it once when he first came back.

He'd not said a lot – the telling was disjointed and upsetting for them both. Enough to make her see that he really just wanted to forget, that he was haunted by the images of all those people starving, roaming around among the utter devastation caused by our own bombs. Once he got back into civvies he'd closed down somehow, and behaved rather as if she and Gemma were strange relations. There'd been some money, and short letters for a couple of years, but after that, nothing. She's going to have to get a bit of a job soon or let out the little box room upstairs. Maybe she can use the typing and shorthand she got from the commercial college. It was just as well that she'd decided to go in that year after grammar school, before she and Donald got married. She'll check the noticeboard in the post office and see if there's anything part-time that would fit in with school hours.

Gemma hadn't paid Donald any attention, other than a slight puzzlement, when he was here and didn't seem bothered when he was gone. At first, Elizabeth had kept up a pretence for her daughter and the neighbours, that Donald was still working away, but after a while there wasn't much point. How little impact he'd had on their lives! So much of this sort of thing after all the cheering and dancing around in 1945. And poor Sarah Crawley, still hoping her Yvonne would turn up again. Elizabeth guesses that the girl either went off to the States with a Yank, or caught it in London in a raid. A neighbour had seen her up there in late summer in '44, somewhere near Piccadilly, but since then, nothing. She catches herself using that word again. *Nothing.* but it was true. During the war people just disappeared into thin air. Nothing to see except a rapidly shrinking picture in the mind.

For a while, although Gemma and Kenny grow taller, their small faces hardly change shape and they are recognisable to everyone and each other. When they are eleven, they have to change schools. The grammar school for boys is right next to the one for girls and they usually catch sight of each other on the long walk to the bus stop, but it is a sharp slice through their shared lives. There are uniforms, and things like science and French, which Gemma loves and Kenny doesn't. There are too many different teachers for him to feel comfortable, not like in the juniors. Too many names and faces for him to remember. He keeps wishing Gemma was there to help him. And, of course, there is homework. Granny Sarah wants to help the boy, but she only stayed at school until she was twelve, so she's a bit at a loss and feels ashamed of her ignorance. She notices his look of disappointment when she gets in a muddle with his arithmetic or composition spelling.

Elizabeth had enjoyed her time at the grammar school, and although now she feels tired at the end of a day's work in the office, she still makes sure there is a routine for Gemma to get homework done on the scrubbed kitchen table before supper. When Kenny comes round to call Gemma out to play, he starts to feel that uncomfortable grumbling in his head, somewhere behind his eyes, when she says she can't go because of homework. Sometimes she has a friend there. A girl called Julie, in the same brown uniform skirt and cardigan. He hears them laughing. He has rushed his schoolwork and now she doesn't even want to see him. He kicks stones all the way back to his house.

Months go past like the wind. When Gemma sees Kenny one weekend, she can't quite think what is different. There's the spot on his chin. Is that it? Or is it his scowl when he looks down at her and she realises how much he's grown? When she says, 'Shall we go and find Champ and take him to the park?' he says yes, but doesn't look at her, just mumbles so she can't hear what he's saying. One day when she knocks at his house, he doesn't answer. She hears thumping, unfamiliar music coming from the upstairs window. The puzzlement skips across her forehead.

Gemma is enjoying school. As the months fly past, she makes lots of friends. Sees Kenny most days on the way to school but not in her kitchen any more.

'Gemma,' says her mum one day, 'I have a feeling Mrs Crawley isn't managing too well. What's that Kenny up to these days? His granny seems a bit down.'

'Think she's OK. Don't know, Mum. Why?'

'Hard for her with a growing lad at her age.' Of course, he won't remember his mum, Elizabeth thinks. He would be too little to understand, but still. She must ask Sarah again if she has ever managed to find the right words to tell Kenny his story in some simple way. 'Why don't you call in and ask them both over on Saturday for tea, dear?'

On Saturday they do come for tea, but it feels awkward. Sarah looks tired, and although she's brought over a small cake she's made, it is a bit stale as if she's just taken it out of a cupboard. Elizabeth notices the boy's hair has grown long. At the front and the back. And he smells a bit sweaty. There are small damp patches under the arms of his T-shirt. Trying to ease the atmosphere, she gets Gemma to show him a piece of art homework that she had got good marks for. It is a sketch of her friend Julie. Kenny sniffs and says she's made the girl even uglier than she is in real life, which feels, to Gemma, like a slap.

Sometimes, for Gemma, the years seem to be racing past like a speeded-up film. She misses Kenny on the days when he is absent and is pleased when she hears his voice from the back of the bus, or ahead of her on the street, but he is usually surrounded by equally noisy boys. He has almost stopped saying hello. Often, she hears his crowd swearing or laughing in an unkind way. She gets used to being ignored by him, but, just occasionally, if he stops to speak to her in the bus queue his voice catches at something inside her. When her friends say giggling, admiring things about Kenny, she can't help but look at him with their eyes. Notices the way his face has changed shape. No longer so rounded – eyes deeper, darker, searching as he scans faces. She feels drawn to his features in spite of herself. He can sometimes take her by surprise with a hello that has echoes of past moments but is in a deeper key. When he looks very directly at her, she feels she'd like to hide. But looks for him when he's not there. When he isn't around she misses something. Distracts herself with her studies. Exams are imminent. When she takes a break from revising, there is always Julie to talk to about the latest film at the Gaumont, and the Hollywood stars in the magazines: their looks, make-up, hairstyles and their love lives.

In 1960, when September comes around again, and a new term begins, Kenny isn't there at all. Not on the school bus. Not walking up the long road, scuffing his shoes, half-empty rucksack swinging from one shoulder. He has had to get a job. The garage in the next street was looking for a young lad to help out and maybe learn the ropes and Mrs Crawley needed the money. And to tell the truth, the school aren't sorry to see the back of this moody and troublesome boy. Gemma gets a glimpse of him when she walks past the garage but he doesn't usually look up. She feels the gap. On her walk to school, the absence of the chance to catch sight of his familiar figure in the distance takes something from her. There is still the noise of swearing and shouting boys on the long road from school to bus but Kenny's voice is missing and she realises how much she has listened out for him each school day for years.

Time passes as it does in adolescence, sometimes too quickly, sometimes at a crawl. Kenny, reaching eighteen, is feeling increasingly awkward in his own skin. He hasn't had a proper girlfriend yet but looks sideways at the ones he sees on the seafront, at the skating rink, and in the shops. And he is overwhelmed, and sometimes appalled by his dreams at night, lying in his narrow bed in the tiny house. His young body has grown so quickly that he feels too big for Sarah's little house. Feeling confined, he goes for fast walks along the seafront, throws pebbles at seagulls, tries to lose himself in the to and fro of the waves. Loud music helps. Secret smoking helps. What he loves best is the roller-skating rink in the middle of Southsea Common; can lose his strange discomforts when he's on a long fast glide, weaving in and out of the slow ones still struggling to stay upright, his head full of the music blaring from the rink's speakers. Sometimes he spots a nice-looking girl watching him. One day he captures a memory for a moment, of those radio lessons in infant school, but now he doesn't feel silly as he moves in swirls, in every direction, to the beat of the music. But hiring roller-skates costs money and he is giving most of his small wage to Granny Sarah each week for housekeeping, so he can't go every week.

It's an unusually chilly and blustery May when a neighbour knocks on the front door to ask Kenny if he could do with a bit of extra cash to wash his car. He's not keen at first, but agrees, keen on some extra money but also looking for any excuse to get out of the house, where Granny Sarah's anxious questions and her new frailty are getting him down. He is surprised to find, once he gets started on the task, that the slip of the cloth and the shine of the clean metal and glass soothes him. And it pays for a skating session. He offers to do it again the next week. One day, while he's doing a final polish of the man's old black Morris, a fancy red car draws up. Kenny whistles to himself. He knows about cars and this is a Jaguar, and it is one of the newer models. A window quietly slides down next to him.

'You look like you're doing a good job there, young man.'

She's blonde, and the car is expensive, and he can't quite work out her voice. She speaks English, but it sounds odd. 'Do you do cars for the others? It looks like you know what to do.' As she speaks, her face lights up with a red-lipped smile. He gets a drift of a new smell. Spicy, musky. The smile fades as he finds himself staring for longer than is polite. She's staying on the seafront in a hotel, the Saville, she tells him, and the car will be parked nearby and she will pay him well if he does a good job. He says he'll be round the next afternoon after work. He thinks of the skating he'll be able to pay for and, just for a moment, about the smell that had reached him from the car window.

The next day, he rushes from work to get there, carrying his bucket and rags and soap, aware of his oily hands and T-shirt, damp with the day's sweat. He probably smells a bit, but there's no time to go home first for a wash. She's there, standing on the hotel steps. For a moment he thinks she looks like one of those film stars, with her blonde hair blowing a little in the breeze, a rainbow of soft material round her shoulders and neck. She quickly joins him, her high-heeled shoes clicking on the pavement as she takes him to where the car is parked, in a yard at the back of the Saville, where there is an outside tap. Bending over, to fill his bucket, he tries to pay attention to the level of water as it rises, but is distracted. The woman seems to be standing very near him. Near enough for him to smell her perfume which makes his head swim a little.

Her car certainly needs a big clean; has splashes of reddish dirt on the wheel hubs. She says it is the rich red earth of Devon, where she's been buying and selling things. She stands, smoking her cigarette, like women he has seen in the movies. He feels her watching him as he cleans, as he bends down to rinse and squeeze the rag, as he stretches over the bonnet to reach the other side of the windscreen; as he straightens up to give a final polish to the roof. He is not sure if he likes being watched like this, especially as he is aware that his T-shirt, which is now too small for him, is riding up above his waist as he stretches across the bonnet.

She says she is pleased. Again, the red lips smile at him. 'And now you can show me the seafront. You should leave the bucket and things here. Collect them later.'

It sounds more like an instruction than a request, in spite of the smile. They walk over to the promenade and sit in a shelter, looking out to sea. Kenny takes the offered cigarette. She is from Sweden, she tells him. Kenny, feeling awkward and excited at the same time, tells her how much he likes her red car.

'Yes. I had to pay some extra to get it in the red but I like it that it means people always remember me. Well, I studied at a very good art school in Stockholm and I designed a lot of marvellous clothes. I like exciting, colourful things. Like my car.' Another smile.

'It's a fantastic car. I've never seen one before, except in the magazines at the garage.' She has turned round to face him and, holding the end of the rainbow scarf towards his hands, asks him to touch it. He feels confused and doesn't quite understand what she wants him to do.

'Go on, Kenny. Feel it. Tell me what you think of my scarf.' And she is doing that looking thing again. That direct stare. And the red-lipped smile.

'I like the colours,' says Kenny, a bit breathlessly. 'And it's very soft, isn't it?' He's never seen anything like it. And he's never touched a grown woman's clothes before, except maybe Granny's ironing. He's never seen a piece of a material like it. It seems to glow with all the colours like the glimmering wings of a butterfly. He remembers going with his school class once to see a room full of moths and butterflies in a little museum near the seafront. He'd been so entranced that he'd nearly got left behind and the teacher had to send a child back to tug at his sleeve.

'Yes, this is one of my own designs. It is the only one like it in the world. I enjoyed making such things when I was studying in Stockholm. But after art school I wanted to travel around Europe and this was so exciting. So different from Sweden. So much more light and colour, you have no idea, especially the further south you go. I began to pick interesting things up here and there. So now I buy antiques and sell them. I like beautiful things, Kenny, my dear.'

When she looks at him directly, holding his gaze, everything else seems to disappear except her blue-grey eyes. When she asks him to tell her his own story, these eyes are searchlights. He doesn't know what to say. He is acutely aware of his breathing. And then a scrap of a memory.

His grandmother had started to tell him something when he was about ten years old, but it hadn't made any sense and since then he had just put it to the back of his mind. He remembers the day that she had called him into her bedroom and sat him down next to her on the bed, and had spoken, out of the blue and all in a rush, about his father who had been a very brave sailor in the Royal Navy and had drowned in a battle before he was born. And his mum had to go away to do important war work somewhere in London. And that was it. She had got up and gone down to the kitchen and put the kettle on and he just knew he was not supposed to ask anything else.

Now the questions he never asked his grandmother, never wanted to think about, roar to the top of his consciousness. Getting up suddenly, he walks off but hears the Swedish woman calling him. She hasn't given him his money yet, she reminds him. Turning back, he mumbles a thank you as she hands him some crisp notes. It is much more than he was expecting and he takes it without looking her in the eyes – avoids the searchlights – blacks out all the inside questions.

'And I am Marit,' she calls after him. 'You must call me Marit. And don't forget to collect your bucket.'

The next day at work the money is burning a hole in his pocket. As soon as he is out, he's sprinting in the direction of the common and the skating rink. Spinning around the central bandstand, whirling across the smooth space, dodging the nervous and irritating slowcoaches, the loud music quietens his troubled mind.

On the next Sunday, Kenny wakes up from a darkly exciting dream and makes breakfast restlessly. Manages to take a cup of tea upstairs to Granny Sarah. Tells her he's off out. She asks if he can get some eggs and potatoes from the corner shop on his way back. Soon he's fast striding along the seafront. The tide is noisily high on the pebbles, the waves full of animation from an angry wind. His cigarette smoke blows about in his face, and he wishes he'd put on his jumper.

And there he sees her. Marit, sitting in the same seaside shelter. Holding herself very still, smiling that enigmatic smile, a large-collared, dark-green raincoat over her shoulders. The rainbow scarf frames her face, wrapped elegantly, holding her hair in place. She beckons to him, patting the seat beside her and, in spite of himself, he finds he cannot retreat or pass by. Soon, he is by her side on the bench, listening, as if drawn by a thread of magic. As she speaks to him, Granny Sarah's eggs and potatoes are quite forgotten.

Later that afternoon, Gemma is walking back from the bus stop with Julie. They are discussing the film they have just seen. Ahead they see the familiar figure of Kenny sloping along, hands stuffed in trouser pockets, looking completely lost in his own thoughts. He's smoking. She wishes he would stop and talk. Inside her head Gemma catches at the edge of something…a sudden scent of buddleia and brick dust, the flop of a damp, dog-worn tennis ball on a wall, the clip of an old bat, the sound of worn plimsoles on her mum's kitchen floor. Sees the welcoming smile of Mrs Crawley, smells a fruit cake freshly out on the kitchen table, and thinks, 'when did I last see Granny Sarah?' She decides to go around to Kenny's later, and invite herself in.

At the door, Mrs Crawley looks pleased, but she is looking older, thinner. Kenny says hello but avoids looking Gemma in the eye. He seems to be uncomfortable seeing Gemma there, even though she's spent so much time in this house over the years. Soon after accepting a cup of tea, feeling awkward, she pleads homework as an excuse to leave. On the way back across the street she feels she has lost something.

It's a week later. On Saturday afternoon, Gemma is heading for the Co-op when she sees Kenny up ahead. The air is clear and sharp. He has got his old school rucksack on his back, and is standing by the bus shelter. There is not much traffic – not unusual. She wants to call out, to wave, but the noise of a car approaching distracts her as it comes racing past them. A red saloon pulls up ahead and the driver gets out; a blonde woman with dark glasses, in a dark-green raincoat, big collar nearly covering her ears. Kenny hasn't seen Gemma because his eyes are on the car. Before she has a chance to call out, she sees him run across to it and the woman is smiling up at him, patting the golden pleated hair at the back of her head. Even from this distance, Gemma sees the glinting of a chunky metal bracelet on the woman's wrist. Is she asking him the way to somewhere? But no, because now she is stroking Kenny's hair before getting back into the driver's seat. Kenny is leaning right into the car. As the passenger door opens, he gets in. The car moves off at speed up the road and out of view. It all happens so quickly. Gemma, puzzled and annoyed, goes home and tries to get on with her work for her exams, but a question in her head won't go away.

Kenny doesn't come home that night. Hasn't been seen at the garage since he'd finished up and left for the day. No one knows where he is. He is in none of his usual haunts. Not at the skating rink. Not down anywhere near the Parade or Southsea Castle, or the fairground at Clarence Pier. The next day, Elizabeth lets a distraught Sarah into the kitchen and makes a pot of tea. As they sit at the kitchen table, it is clear Kenny's granny is at her wits' end. Sitting on the stairs in the hallway, Gemma listens to the cracked voice squeezed out between sobs. She's not been good enough, she says. Kenny has suffered, not knowing his mother. Old history. Lots of people in the same boat after the war. She's done her best, but she's failed him. He's nearly a man now and she supposes he'll look after himself. He's never been the same since going to big school.

During the next few days, the police make an effort to look for him. They distribute a photo, ask at railway stations, the usual sort of thing. Sarah Crawley seems too distressed to talk about it but, encouraged by Elizabeth, Gemma has made a statement to the police, but 'he's not a child,' they say. 'He is eighteen and boys his age do go off,' they say. 'A blonde woman?' they say, 'He'll be back before you know it,' they say. She tries to remind everyone again about the fancy red car but she's not sure if people pay attention. She has an urge to join the hunt for her childhood playmate. But through the kitchen door, as she looks across at Mrs Crawley's face, she thinks Kenny's granny has drawn a thick, black line under her old friend. As if she has expected this to happen. Had always known it would.

When, after a couple of months, a postcard arrives from Kenny, saying not to worry, Sarah Crawley feels it's just like the note his mum had left for her in '44, but at least this card has a picture on one side. She reads it again and again until she has it by heart, before putting it in the kitchen drawer under the paisley lining paper.

> *Dear Granny, Please don't worry about me. I am fine. I have a good job as a gardener and am learning my trade. I am in a great big place in Yorkshire. I will try and write again. Thank you for all you have done for me. Love from your Kenny.*

Part Three

Where to Now?

Afterwards, Kenny couldn't remember making the decision. He didn't know why he'd agreed, why he'd got into the car. Because he'd been scared of her, disturbed by the eyes, the questions, even her perfume. Sitting with Marit again on that last morning in the seaside shelter, watching the roaring waves, he'd tried to follow a single, rushing seagull in its pursuit of nothing, as a way of holding onto his own flying thoughts as she talked in that not-quite-English way. Her questions felt like a blinding light, and he wanted to stay in the dark. What was most frightening was not how many of her questions were unanswerable, it was the dawning realisation that he'd never properly asked himself in all these years why he'd never heard talk of a mother, a father, any family, other than that scrap of a conversation he'd not understood with Granny Sarah when he was ten. Another image had quickly followed this one into his consciousness. Gemma, playing hopscotch outside her house, not long after her father had turned up, had said 'Is your daddy going to come back from the war now, Kenny?' and he'd just thrown down the stone he was holding and run off home. She'd never asked again.

And then, sitting in the shelter with the wind whistling off the sea, Marit had started talking very quietly to him in that slightly foreign, husky voice about where she lived. A grand house with beautiful grounds and fantastic views of the hills all around, somewhere up in the north. Too much to manage for her elderly head gardener. And she was away a lot these days with her antique's business.

'The place needs someone. Someone younger, someone stronger,' she'd said, looking directly into Kenny's eyes till he felt dizzy. 'What are you doing now?' she went on. 'Hanging round an oily, smelly garage for next to nothing? You could come and learn a real skill, and you'd be in the fresh air. Landscape gardening is a proper thing, Kenny, with a future and I know you would settle in there very comfortably. In my house. With me.' He'd looked away from her, turned his eyes out to sea, watching the ferry struggling a little on its way to Ryde Pier. 'I can teach you so much,' she'd said. 'And we could have such fun.' Then he'd felt the softness of her hand as it rested on his. And he'd shivered.

That night he'd struggled with the fighting thoughts. Dreadful dreams full of thrown-about images: Granny shouting at him, a massive high sea coming over the top of the shelter, the skating rink full of soldiers with guns. In the morning he'd stuffed a few clothes into his old school rucksack. Standing by his door, looking around the familiar old room, he'd caught sight of the book Gemma had given him for his tenth birthday.

Hans Christian Andersen's stories. He'd not read all of them – wasn't as quick a reader as her – but one or two had stayed in his mind. And Gemma's home-made card was still inside the book. On an impulse he'd stuffed it among the socks and jeans and T-shirts. After taking Granny Sarah her usual cup of tea, he'd called goodbye, as if he was going off to the garage as usual, hadn't waited for her to come down in her dressing gown to kiss him on the cheek like she always wanted to. He couldn't face that today. Because she was used to his grumpiness in the mornings, he hoped she would put it down to that. As soon as work finished, he set off to the agreed meeting point. To wait for Marit to drive by and pick him up.

After she put her warm hand on the back of his head, he got into the car. She passed him a hand-rolled cigarette with a sweetish taste, then leaned over to cover him with a large, soft, woollen blanket. The car sped on through the downs. The light was fading and he was soon sleeping. When he half woke, he realised he was listening to some extraordinarily soothing music, and catching the spicy drift of her perfume, he slept again. His memories of the rest of the journey are vague. Another hand-rolled cigarette, sips of something delicious from a silver flask, a couple of stops, at a petrol station for fuel, at a roadside café for coffee and a piece of cake, a seemingly never-ending line of lorries that needed overtaking and then fewer lights, fewer vehicles, an empty road, a sense of rising ground. He drifted in and out of sleep, half aware of the rough stone walls either side of the car. Then in the distance the shadowy shape of a large building behind higher walls loomed up out of the mist that was hovering over the narrow road. He must have briefly slept again as the red car drove between tall gates. It was the sudden silence of the stilled car that woke him as the woman leaned over and kissed him, and he knew he had come to heaven.

Waking early next morning he opened his eyes to a half-lit world. It wasn't so much waking up as floating to the surface. Kenny felt as if he had no bones in his body, that he was exactly the perfect temperature, that his limbs were all the perfect length for limbs. Lying on the white-sheeted mattress under a weightless but warm cover of some strange kind, it was as if he lay held gently in a cloud. He slept again.

When he woke next, Marit was there, standing by the side of the bed, looking down at him, her long hair now neatly pinned back from her face. The lips were red again. In the night, her hair had fallen over her face, hiding her expressions from him, but the sounds from her mouth and her movements had shown him how she could be pleased.

Half-sitting up, his tongue felt thick and when he tried to ask her what time it was, the words seemed to cling to the dryness in his mouth. She was gently smoothing his hair back from his forehead, and the drift of something delicious was reaching his nostrils. It was from her skin, the same waft of spice, the invitation his imagination had responded to on the car journey before he'd fallen asleep. And now this scent led him into memories of the night; of the sight of himself naked and outstretched on a huge bed, mirrored in the large wardrobe door, of watching her take off garments slowly, one by one, her eyes never leaving his face, and the feel of her unclothed skin next to his.

Fully awake now, he reached out to touch her face, but she moved back. A flicker of a frown, a slight tightening around the mouth. Looking for a moment like a teacher about to chastise him. How her face could change and then change back. How did this happen? Marit was smiling gently again, but her words were clear. More like a command than an invitation. It was time for him to shower and get dressed, she said. And then he should come downstairs to the big kitchen and, after some breakfast, she would show him all of her amazing estate.

They had arrived in the dark, well after midnight. Images of their arrival flooded Kenny's mind as he threw back the covers and put his feet to the ground, feeling the rich thickness of carpet beneath them. Film-like images of dreamily driving towards the large gates. Of a kiss from heaven. Of stone steps up to a huge door. More stairs, wooden but carpeted, rising from a tiled hallway. He remembers the noise of their feet as they crossed the hall, and then? He must have still been half asleep, was lying in a deep bath (how did he get there?) with gently curved sides and clawed feet. He remembers the feel of her fingers massaging his back and neck, confused to see her in front of him at the same time, before realising that she was reflected in a huge mottled mirror which covered the whole of the wall.

Marit behind him, Marit in front of him. At the same time.

Marit had also stared into the mirror. At first her eyes scanned her own reflection, with admiration. Then they took in the lovely young man, his glowing eyes fixed on her reflection, his skin sleek in the bath water. As the steam rose to blur these images, she smiled with the anticipation of sweet pleasure.

Seated at an oak table in a vast tiled kitchen, Kenny was served silently by a grey-haired woman in a large, starched apron. On a colourfully decorated plate in front of him there were deliciously creamy scrambled eggs with some sort of cold orange fish. He'd never eaten anything like it ever before and was surprised at how good these two things tasted together. And the dark-green, gold-rimmed cup of coffee he was holding in both hands was unlike anything he'd had at home. Granny Sarah always just put a spoonful of Nescafé from the jar into a mug and poured on hot water, before adding a splash of milk and a spoonful of sugar. The smell of this rich dark brew was extraordinary. He had caught a drift of it as he'd been coming down the stairs after getting showered and dressed.

He was wearing his clothes from yesterday, which he'd found, miraculously washed and dried, on the chair by his bed. As he bent slightly to put a forkful of creamy egg into his mouth, he felt Marit's hand on the back of his neck. Startled, he jumped slightly, and his fork clattered noisily onto the flagstone floor. How could she move about so silently?

'Enjoying breakfast, my sweet?' she asked, passing him a clean fork and sitting opposite him at the table. 'You look like you are relishing the smoked salmon. And what do you think about my china?' He managed to nod, his mouth still full of egg. 'I told you how I love beautiful things. I hope you feel the same way. I found these old platters in a marvellous little market in Provence.' He looked a little blank. 'It's in the far south of France, my sweet, and it is one of my favourite places to visit. So unlike Sweden! Maybe I will take you there one day.' She performed a smile as if her eyes were feasting on him. 'Carry on. But I do want you to finish quickly so that I can take you to the outside and introduce you to my realm. Is that the word in English?'

Kenny hurriedly scraped the last forkful into his mouth and wiped a hand across his lips. As he did so, he caught the briefest of disapproving frowns on Marit's face.

'There is a little washroom behind that grey door over there. Go quickly now, Kenny dear, and wash your hands and face and we'll go outside into the lovely morning sunshine.'

Feeling the warm water running through his soapy fingers, he looked in the mirror over the basin and stared for a moment at his face. It stared back. He had until now assumed that, since growing to his full height, his features were a constant. He'd always been recognised, by Granny, by Mrs Siddons, by his teachers, by the garage owner, by Gemma, but this seemed a different Kenny looking back at him, and he knew that something had changed forever. He was now in Marit's world, and her face, he thought, was like a sheet of water. Able to reflect the glow of sunset, as it had on their drive last evening, but also to melt in pleasure, seen in the half-light before dawn today. Now he had seen it ripple in a second, blown by some small wind of discontent. He stared again into the mirror until he heard her calling.

'Come along, Kenny, my sweet. My garden is waiting for us.'

As Marit pulled open the garden door, letting the light flood in, he realised how dark the kitchen had been. Feeling Marit's hand take his, he followed her out. In the bright daylight he noticed her dress. It had a silky sheen and, like the scarf she'd worn as they sat in the seaside shelter – was it only last week? – it had many colours. Its wide sleeves covered her arms and the skirt swept over her hips to her knees.

He heard and felt his shoes crunch along the gravel path. As they rounded the corner of the house, Marit stopped. Kenny was stunned by what he could see. Of course, they'd got here in the dark. Now the mile upon mile of intense green of the fields took his breath away. Back home, the only green to be seen was Southsea Common where the roller-skating rink stood, surrounded by over-trodden flat grass, intersected by tarmac paths lined with stunted trees. Here, the lush fields were made into a patchwork by old stone walls, and the lines of these walls seemed to draw his eyes on to the distant hills. He imagined, with a sliver of anxiety, how easy it would be to get lost here. How would he know in which direction to go? In Southsea you always knew which way you were pointing because the sea and the beach and the pier were to the south and the South Downs were to the north and on each side of the town lay a harbour.

'Come, Kenny,' he heard her voice calling him. She had moved further down the path. Feeling summoned, he quickly joined her and felt a rush of excitement as she took his hand again, leading him on between wide beds of flowers.

'Morning, madam.' An old man in dungarees put down his wheelbarrow, a tweed cap shading his eyes from the sun.

'Bert, this is Kenny and, as I told you, he will replace Stephen, who left last month, so he's going to help you with the rougher tasks and is going to need to learn everything from you. Pass on all your wisdom, please, Bert dear!' And she gave the man a smile that lasted a little longer than seemed natural. 'Kenny, this is Bert who I rely on completely. He was already here when I bought the Hall and knows everything about the things that grow well here and the things that are not worth bothering about.'

'Yes, madam.' Bert raised a hand to his cap, not quite in a salute, but Kenny pictured an old retainer from the last century making a similar gesture to a lord or lady of the manor.

'Very nice to meet you, Bert,' Kenny said. He noticed a quizzical – or amused – scanning of him by the old eyes. Marit's hand drew him on, past Bert and the wheelbarrow,

66

towards the enclosing stone wall of the garden, over which Kenny could see for miles. He felt another small shiver of uncertainty at the prospect of getting lost. He had once thought he'd been abandoned on the seafront when he was about five. He'd got separated from Granny and the others in the crowds for a moment, and in his panic among all the tall strangers going every which way, he had gone in the wrong direction. It was as if the whole world had become a dangerous place in which he would never again be found, until his loud sobbing led his friend Gemma and her mother to his side.

The sudden touch of Marit's warm hand on the back of his neck brought him back to the present.

'Come, sweetheart, come out from your dreaming. Come back to me,' she said, so quietly that he hardly heard her words. And they turned back towards the house along the paths, past the stands of tall flowers. Back at the kitchen door, she turned to him.

'Well, this will be better than your oil-and-grease garage, don't you think?'

He found himself searching her face, seeking some reminder of the softness he'd seen in the night. He wanted a sign that all that hadn't been just a dream. When she lifted and held one of his hands to her cheek, and then to her mouth, he wanted to be back there, under the soft quilt, covered by her warm body in the dark.

'Tomorrow I am going to leave you in Bert's capable hands, my sweet. Capability Bert,' she smiled at him, but he didn't know why. 'But now I need to deal with some very boring but important business in my office so please explore by yourself. Wander around a bit with Bert, and learn the geography of the gardens so that you won't ever get lost if I'm not here to find you.' And smiling, in a Cheshire-cat moment, she was gone.

Standing still, alone, for a moment Kenny felt bereft. Hearing a cry in the sky above him, he looked up to see a large-winged bird soaring towards a group of trees beyond the high wall where he and Marit had been standing. He didn't recognise it. He'd only really known seagulls, sparrows, starlings and the occasional robin. Unsure if he felt dismissed, abandoned or set free, he wondered what rules there might be. Was he supposed to explore, or were there places not allowed? Was Marit someone who could be displeased? He knows he pleased her last night... her small cries...or was it this morning?

The sound of the wheelbarrow broke into his rush of pleasurable memories.

'Well, young lad, p'raps you'll not mind helping me with this? The previous young man usually gave us a hand.'

The barrow was now full of terracotta pots. Bert mumbled that he'd been digging in some bedding plants, 'Now May's nearly out!' The empty pots needed taking to his shed. Glad to be told what to do, Kenny picked up the handles of the barrow and followed Bert along, trying hard to memorise the pattern of the paths. Kenny hoped he wouldn't need a pocketful of breadcrumbs to drop on the path like Hansel in Miss Newey's old storybook, which he'd loved so much.

He had been outside in the grounds all afternoon, helping Bert. He had offered to have a go at some digging and planting, brushed the paths with an enormous broom, and been shown the greenhouses filled with the scent of tomato plants and geranium leaves. But since the old man had gone back to his little house in the grounds for his tea, Kenny had been sitting on a rustic bench in a daze, staring into the distance, trying to piece together the last twenty-four hours. The garage in

Southsea seemed a million miles away, yet it was only yesterday afternoon that he'd changed a set of spark plugs on that old Rover, the last job of the day, before heading off to the bus stop to meet Marit. Then there was that dreamlike journey through the dusk and the dark to their arrival here and to the most amazing night of his life so far. If that was a dream, he wanted more like it. The extraordinary feeling of lying close enough to hear another's breath, to smell their skin. To experience the intensity of her eyes so focused on him, first when she bathed him, and then as she covered him with her own body under that cloud-like quilt, to feel that rising excitement and…

The feel of Marit's hand on the centre of his back made him jump.

'Kenny, my love, you were miles away. Sweet dreamings, I hope?'

Her hand was now drifting across his forehead, brushing his dark hair back, as he turned to look up at her. His memories of the previous night's pleasures merged with the warmth rising up in him from her present touch.

'Yes, Marit, very sweet dreams,' he said, with a smile, as his eyes met her downward gaze. Her blue-grey eyes were hypnotic, and he knew it wasn't just the strange cigarettes and spirits she'd given him that had brought him into this state.

'Well, Kenny, my sweet, time to go inside. Haven't you noticed that the light is fading?' Looking around, he saw that the greens of the distant hills were greying, and that the first faint small star was just visible. Marit, taking his hand as he stood up, brushed his cheek with her lips. 'I have some extremely delicious wine inside that we will taste before supper. But first, because you have been working out here all afternoon, I think a bath will be good for you. You don't want to have sore muscles tomorrow.'

Leaving Home

When she is eighteen, Gemma is offered a university place to study geography. She is beginning to be more interested in places than people and has started to feel an occasional longing for travel. She has spent so many hours over the years at the edge of the sea, staring out at the horizon, watching the ships disappear and trying to picture what they would soon be seeing. Yet she has a confusion inside her head. Part of her really wants to see more of the world, while another voice inside shivers at the thought of leaving her familiar home. She worries that she will always be a person who can't make up her mind about things.

Now life is taking off in a new direction, with many distractions, she forgets Kenny for long periods of time, but he can suddenly enter her headspace in one of those mindless moments, like when washing dishes, dead-heading the last few geraniums in Elizabeth's window boxes, or walking past the site of the old bombed house, now in the process of demolition. In those moments, Gemma recalls the day when Granny Sarah came to the door, all breathless, to tell Elizabeth about the card from Kenny.

'A lovely picture. From Yorkshire. A job as a gardener somewhere up north, he said. On a big estate. Learning a trade. Sent his love.' And Kenny's granny had sat down and cried a bit into her handkerchief while Elizabeth made her a cup of tea.

Gemma is getting ready to leave soon, heading for Birmingham, which she knows from the day of her interview is a huge city of big roads, factories, vast noisy shopping centres and red-brick houses. In the midst of her exciting preparations, a tune, a smell or a dog barking down the street can catch her attention and she can remember Kenny suddenly, viscerally. Where did he go? Why? Does she ever walk into his dreams like he does in hers?

Early on a day at the end of September, Gemma stands looking at herself in the bedroom mirror. Her fair curls are well tucked and pinned under a red check beret. She is wearing a plain white shirt under the new greyish two-piece suit her mother has bought her. Is it a bit tweedy? she wonders, tugging at the bottom of the little jacket. Leaning slightly towards the mirror she tries to persuade her pale, glossy lips into a smile but it doesn't quite work. In the mirror she can see the bedroom behind her. The only place she has ever known. Picking up her suitcase in one hand and the new handbag in the other she turns to go downstairs, heart beating slightly faster than usual.

She leaves on a very early train from the Harbour Station, waving goodbye to a tearful Elizabeth. Settling into a window seat, she watches the familiar sights disappearing one by one, the harbour and ships, the Guildhall Square, then Langstone Harbour, the stranded small boats tipped on one side in the mud, waiting for the return of the tide. For a second, Gemma imagines herself floating out of the carriage window and flying onto one of the boats, imagines the taste of the salty air, the view of the harbour mouth, feels the wind on her face.

Where is the excitement, the sense of freedom, of being grown-up, of adventure? All she feels now is a sense of panic, the loss of the familiar, of the known, of being known. Looking around the compartment, she sees only strangers, as strange to her as she is to them. When the train stops at Havant Station, she is ready to get off and catch a train back, back home to Elizabeth, to the small comforts of her childhood world. Gemma has never felt so alone.

Arriving in late afternoon at her new lodgings, she receives an effusively warm welcome from the landlady.

'You must be exhausted after your journey, dear. And I expect changing stations at London was a nightmare, at least it was when I last tried it. You'll come and rest your legs and have a cuppa with me, before I show you the room.'

'Thank you, that will be lovely, Mrs Johnson, but if I could just wash my hands first after the train. You know, everything gets so grubby, specially going across London.'

'Of course, dear, but please call me Beryl, and always feel you can come in for a chat. Anytime.'

Feeling overwhelmed by the size of the city and the height of the buildings in the centre, and the noise of everything, Gemma's glad of Beryl's welcome. In spite of a fluttering anxiety in her stomach and a fog of tension in her head, as the first week goes by, she begins to find her feet, learning the geography of the campus, getting her head around her complicated timetable, and making friends with students on her course. Some of them meet up with her in the student union bar on the first Saturday night. Sandwiched between the noise of raucous rugby songs from one side and the juke box playing on the other, it is impossible to hear what her new friends are saying but she doesn't care. Sipping her beer, she decides it feels wonderful.

As weeks pass by, her landlady's attentions begin to stifle her. The predictability of Beryl's head appearing round the door, whatever time Gemma gets home, is irksome. She is supposed to have a Sunday lunch each week as part of her rent. At first this was a welcome bit of homely comfort.

'How many potatoes, dear? Only two, are you sure? You like my gravy, now, I know. My Sylvia, she was always on about me making plenty of gravy.'

This was often followed by a hanky to the nose, a downward look and a bit of a sniff. Gemma has learned very quickly about Beryl's daughter, Sylvia, the same age as Gemma, who had gone for a daring spin on her boyfriend's new scooter and come off on the Bristol Road dual carriageway, without a helmet of course. She's heard the details many times now. The deadly patch of oil on the road. The time it took for an ambulance to come. The number of hours in a coma. The final sit by the bedside. The funeral. The dealing with Sylvia's clothes, her various strappy shoes, her half-used Rimmel make-up palettes. And then there are the photograph albums. Gemma feels at times that she is as familiar with Sylvia's progress through her short life as her own.

In late October, just as Gemma begins to really enjoy her student life away from home, the world seems suddenly, terrifyingly dangerous. The Cuban Missile Crisis, they call it. The newspapers shout their headlines: 'Blockade!' 'Will there be War?' The American President throws a cordon round the island as Russian ships carrying missiles head directly towards them. Televisions and radios tell the world to hold its breath.

On the night when no one knows if the Russian ships will stop, Beryl and Gemma, both in pyjamas, find each other in the small kitchen at four in the morning, both sleepless with worry. Sitting together, Beryl with her hair in curlers, their hands clasped around mugs of sweetened cocoa, they are glad of each other's company as, according to the news, it looks like World War Three may be about to start. Gemma wonders if Elizabeth is also awake, and pictures her mother sitting at the kitchen table after making cocoa or tea for her and Granny Sarah. And Kenny? Where is he now? Might he be awake somewhere too, while Kennedy's American warships bar the way for the oncoming Russian navy with their cargo of deadly missiles destined for Cuba?

When the crisis has passed, and the Russian ships have turned back, things return to a kind of normal. Gemma realises she is less irritated by Beryl's repetitions and theatrical sniffs. It is also quite possible that Beryl finds less need to talk about the past so much, since their night of shared terror and cocoa. The sense of imminent destruction has brought them both more into the present.

Gemma settles into student life with its mix of lectures, essays, late nights and parties until the fearsomely cold winter of 1962 starts. As her first term away from home ends, Gemma manages to set off for Christmas between snowstorms. Her landlady looks genuinely sad when they say a shivering goodbye on the doorstep, Beryl in her wellington boots over thick socks, an old coat clutched around her dressing gown, Gemma wearing her warmest polo-necked jumper and trousers under a hooded duffle coat. Gemma surprises herself by giving her landlady a light kiss on her cheek before setting off for the bus station.

In January, the snow is still falling, piling up at the sides of the pavements as Gemma lugs her case along from the bus stop back to Beryl's house. The forecast is more of the same for the foreseeable future. Football matches have been cancelled. There are standpipes in the streets. Pipes are frozen nearly everywhere, and Gemma is glad the next day to find the baths in the basement of the Student Union are still available for a proper hot soak.

In the weeks and weeks that follow, Gemma's walks to the bus stop through a monochrome city, the icy pavements edged with piled up packed and dirty snow are treacherous. Nights are so cold that Gemma hunches herself in the narrow bed around hot water bottles under blankets and coats, to wake aching and stiff with cold.

The thaw, when it arrives at last, is extraordinary. Grass appears again from under the snow, trees and shrubs burst into leaf and flower, swathes of brilliant tulips spread across the beds in the parks. Gemma, staring out of the coach window at the green of the countryside on the journey back to Southsea for Easter, feels as if this is the first ever real spring.

Back home, she realises how much she has missed the sea. Why on earth had she chosen a university that was about as far from the sea as one could get? She takes herself out every day to get as much of it as possible, wanting to store it up inside herself: the smell, the noise of it, the way her gaze can reach across to the horizon. One day, striding along, with the pier behind her and Southsea Castle ahead, drinking it all in, a sudden squall stings her face, and she makes for the familiar shelter where the hailstones angrily hit the glass walls. The mass of the Isle of Wight disappears, eaten by the grey smudge of the squall. There is something so comforting about this shelter, not just because of its protection against the worst of the weather but because of the way it is peopled by her childhood friends, and all the picture postcard days of picnics and swimming in the summer sun. A bit of her wants to stay in this shelter forever.

After Easter she reluctantly packs her case and waves goodbye to Elizabeth through the window of her coach back to Birmingham.

At the end of her third term, which is full of lectures, revision, and exams, Gemma is torn between a longing for the comfort of home and a new eagerness for adventure. Instead of going straight back to Southsea, the urge to travel wins out. She can hear the disappointment in Elizabeth's voice when she tells her over the phone but promises to get back to see her well before the start of next term. With exams out of the way she's done a few weeks' part-time work in a big store in the city centre, selling expensive leather and ceramic goods to rich people. She has managed to save a bit and has been able to buy a cheap rucksack, a pair of jeans and some second-hand boots in the market before setting off. She travels on buses and trains. Bravely stops in youth hostels. In one hostel, a vibrantly dressed and ear-ringed young woman called Rosie seeks her out and seems to want to travel with her. When things go missing from

Gemma's rucksack, Rosie at first denies it before admitting angrily her sense of deprivation and envy of Gemma's cosy life story. Gemma has envied Rosie's exotic second-hand clothes and her lack of inhibition but now realises how lucky she has been in childhood. And she thinks again with sadness of Kenny. Where had he gone with that older woman with the blonde hair piled high like a crown on top of her head, who'd screeched to a halt by the bus stop that day in her expensive-looking red car? He'd sent his granny that one card from somewhere in the north to say he was fine, really fine. But then just nothing and a crack had opened up in her life.

Travelling alongside Rosie gets more difficult. Gemma resists the invitation to do some shoplifting, turns down the offered drugs. She leaves quietly, very early one morning while her companion sleeps. At the station she scans the information boards for trains that morning and decides to get a ticket for a station in Yorkshire.

After a long train journey and two bus rides, Gemma goes deeper and deeper into the green of the countryside to the pretty pub in a tiny village where she has managed to book in for bed and breakfast. The man from the tourist office at Darlington has phoned ahead for her. On the last bus ride, she worries it may be too remote. But it is far less gloomy than Birmingham during the holidays and walking by the river before supper on her first evening, Gemma listens to the sound of the water rushing over stones, smells the fresh sweetness of the air, listens to the distant sheep calling to each other, and catches the swoop of bats and decides she loves it.

Eating in the bar on her second evening, she gets into conversation with a crowd of hikers staying there that night. They recommend a visit to a stately home in the region.

'Coldwater Hall. It's an absolutely ancient pile,' says one of the boys, the one with the pink shirt and flopped fringe.

'The gardens are glorious and the gardener drop-dead gorgeous,' says the youngest of the girls, fluttering her eyelashes.

'But so sad,' chips in a rather plainer and more serious-looking girl. 'I think the boss woman keeps him under lock and key,'

'Is she his mother?' asks Gemma.

'No way,' scoffs the fringe. 'Not going by how she patted his backside and the way he winced. More like a sex slave if you ask me.'

'God, Freddy,' says the pretty one, 'you have a one-track mind.'

When an upsurge of voices from the dartboard corner crashes over them like a tsunami of sound, the conversation at Gemma's small table moves on to where the group will go next. To head off to catch a train to Scotland or to stay and climb the stone-wall clad hillsides to the next dale? Gemma's head swims a little with the beer and the swirling voices and decides to call it a day.

Late down to breakfast next morning, heavy-headed and dry-mouthed, she looks for her companions of the night before, but they have already gone. She toys with the plate of local sausage, bacon and eggs, sips her coffee then discards her toast and marmalade. Cold dankness seeps out into her solitary mood. She misses them. Their absence, after the sense of connection she'd felt the previous evening, brings thoughts again of Kenny. He had seemed such a permanent and warm part of her life until they moved to secondary school. The gradual change in him then. The way he'd started to pass by without saying hello, surrounded by his gang of noisy boys. Often absent, but the centre of any kerfuffle in the streets near the school when he was there.

For a while he'd started to acknowledge her again. It would have been when she was about fifteen. She'd glowed when she felt his attention on her, but then his brown eyes would shift in another direction and she'd lose him all over again. When he was no longer at school, she had sometimes found herself strolling past the garage where he was working, hoping to bump into him, but if that happened, she'd be lost for words and would feel a warm flush rising to her cheeks.

'More coffee, my love? Breakfast too much for you today?' The waitress's smiling face splits Kenny's image and she is back facing her half-eaten, congealing breakfast.

'Sorry. Too much of your lovely beer last night I think,' she says. 'Maybe I need fresh air and exercise. How do I get to Coldwater Hall? Some people last night were telling me to give it a visit.'

The waitress's smile flies out of the window. 'Well, OK. It is a stunning place but—'

'But what?'

'Hard to say really… It is a fine old place with a marvellous view – quite a way from here, mind, and, well, to tell you the truth, I've heard that the owner isn't well liked in the neighbourhood. Something about her. High-handed and a woman of few words. She turned up a few years ago and bought the manor, with cash, they say. She's some kind of foreigner. But if you like gardens, then why not give it a try.'

'Yes, of course. And maybe I'll go a bit easier on your lovely beer tonight so I can enjoy my breakfast tomorrow.'

Gemma packs her rucksack, trying to capture the wisp of an elusive thought at the back of her mind… Was it something about home? But it's gone, like the last drift of a dream's smoke when you have been woken suddenly. She decides on impulse to use the red telephone box in the village square to call her mother. When she hears that Granny Sarah has died, she feels tears on her cheeks.

'You will come for the funeral,' Elizabeth says.

Gemma looks out of the smeary train window, unable to concentrate on either her paperback Jane Austen or the news in her paper. Profumo, Dr Stephen Ward, Christine Keeler... What was that all about? She'd not properly read a paper since before her exams so the names were just names. She watches the stone-walled bright green fields of sheep pass, thinking how Granny Sarah will not be there when she gets home. Will Kenny come? she wonders, watching the world go by. More and more buildings, less and less space. Smoke billowing out of huge factory chimneys. Gemma shuts her eyes and is soon sleeping.

The world gets much noisier when she reaches London and has to get across to Waterloo Station. The platform for Portsmouth Harbour is full of travellers hurrying in their own bubble of anxiety, families joyfully meeting up with loud cries and frantic waves, or couples saying sad goodbyes, holding each other in silent farewells. Finding a seat on her train, she gratefully sinks down and soon sleeps, waking only when the train passes through Havant.

As she pulls into the final station, she catches sight of the familiar harbour views and for a rushing moment is glad to be back. Heaving her heavy rucksack over one shoulder, she gets off the train, and after a short bus ride to the end of her terrace, she is home. Elizabeth is waving from the front window, before rushing to open the door, arms out ready. Gemma and her mother are both fighting back tears and are soon sitting at the kitchen table to look at each other. Then the questions, all coming out at once, each to the other.

'Where have you been?'

'What happened to Sarah?'

'Can you stay for a bit, now you are here?'

'Has anyone heard from Kenny?'

'You must want something to eat!'

'When is the funeral?'

And then silence. Until Elizabeth gets up and cuts bread, spreads margarine, slices cheese. Gemma gets up and puts the kettle on to boil.

Later, upstairs in her familiar old room, she unpacks the rucksack. Takes out the Jane Austen and the Ian Fleming, a bag of washing things, a few pairs of knickers and a spare bra, creased shorts, a pair of slightly grubby jeans, two T-shirts and a cardigan. She's left her walking boots and heavy waterproof jacket at the Yorkshire pub. Right at the bottom, in a paper bag, is her only proper dress, bought in the sales out of her last wage packet. A new make by a designer called Mary Quant. Very short, black with a wide white lacy collar. Gemma gives it a sniff and decides it will do for the funeral. Again, wonders if Kenny will be there. Surely, he must be. He must know, somehow, that Sarah is going to be buried.

In the Siddons's front room, the voices are quiet after the bleak short service and burial. Elizabeth had said a few tearful words in the church, but realises how much she didn't really know about her dear old friend. There are big gaps. And today a very obvious gap. No, Kenny has not come. No one had any idea how to contact him.

Familiar faces from the street and from Sarah's church sip

the sherry that Elizabeth has provided, to go with a shop-bought fruit cake and some cucumber and ham sandwiches from Sarah's next-door neighbours. There have been a few changes in the street in the last year so there are unfamiliar faces too, come to pay their neighbourly respects. And suddenly there is Gemma's old friend Julie. No longer in the brown school uniform with pigtailed hair but floating into the room in a silk paisley kaftan and little white Courrèges boots. Gemma feels a huge gust of pleasure, in spite of the seriousness of the occasion, and they clutch each other, exclaiming questions in hushed but excited tones.

As the sherry gets passed around, the general chatter gets louder and suddenly there is someone very tall bending down to Gemma's level to talk to her.

'Bruce. My name's Bruce. Just moved in down the street.'

He's an engineering student, he says, here in Portsmouth, at the college and he's got digs down the road with a family who had a spare room. He is lightly freckled, and has rather short and coarse reddish hair, but his voice, rich and deep, (and a bit posh, Gemma thinks), doesn't match any of this and nor do his blue eyes. She takes the glass of sherry he is offering her and she just wants him to go on speaking.

Prince Charming

Gemma had planned to get straight back to her walking adventure in Yorkshire, had intended only staying for a few days in Southsea to help Elizabeth sort out Sarah's little house but found herself held there by invisible threads until it was time to return to Birmingham for the start of term.

After the funeral, Elizabeth had been shocked to discover how very little was left in Sarah's house. I should have kept more of an eye on her, she thought. There had been a will made long ago when Sarah's husband had died leaving everything to Yvonne. Sarah had never made another, but that was no matter because she had nothing to leave. Of course, she'd paid regularly into a funeral club, so the cost of her simple burial was covered. The man who came to take away her bits of furniture said, with a sniff, that it was hardly worth his while. The solicitor had asked Elizabeth, as the person who had known Sarah the longest, to oversee the house clearance. She should keep anything she wanted as payment for her trouble. Elizabeth took the pretty, blue glass dishes from the bedroom table and a green cake tin to remind her of Sarah. And for some reason the framed wedding photo of Sarah and Cyril that had surprised her. She'd never seen this picture before. Where on earth had Sarah kept it hidden and why?

'The men from Browns have been there with their van to clear the house before the new people move in, but I want to do a final clean up,' Elizabeth told Gemma one morning, a few days after the funeral. 'And no, I don't need help with that. I want to be sure everything's left hunky-dory, Gemma dear. But I've got behind with things here, what with work, and the funeral do, and one thing and another, so if you can tidy things up a bit in the kitchen and upstairs, while I'm seeing to things at Sarah's, that'd be no end of help. And tomorrow I can take you out for a little lunch.'

'Yes, Mum, no problem,' Gemma said, squashing the pictures in her mind of the welcoming evenings in the warm Yorkshire pub, the view in the early mornings of sheep meandering around the field opposite her little window.

'To be honest, Sarah had let things go in the last year or two. Ever since Kenny… Well, let's just say Sarah lost interest and so things went downhill. The state of the place along with her spirits.'

'Oh Mum, I wish I'd realised,' said Gemma, thinking of all those things she'd not paid attention to, too busy in her new world.

'I can't remember when I last had one of Sarah's cakes,' Elizabeth said quietly, almost as if to herself. 'No chance now, for sure.'

Gemma continued drying the plates, but hearing the sadness in her mother's voice, echoing her own regret, she thought that maybe she should stay home a bit longer. Although there'd been a big age gap, Sarah Crawley had always been there across the road, like family, a daily presence in her mum's life.

That afternoon, after finishing off the chores, Gemma found herself walking along the seafront, seeking the bite of the wind and the noisy distraction of waves on the pebbles. Sitting in the old seaside shelter that day, focusing on the horizon, idly counting the vessels, she remembered how, as a child, she'd been taught to look at the way ships would start to disappear as they reached the line between sea and sky. She'd been fascinated at the notion of the earth being actually round; wasn't sure she could believe it; her imagination told her that the ships must be falling over the edge.

Walking back to her old home, she'd tried to gather the cobwebs in her head into some kind of order. She'd always known that she was bright and had done well at school. Now it felt as if her brain had stopped working properly. It felt clogged up with unfinished thoughts, unsaid sentences, half-formed questions. And in several of these questions was the name Kenny. Hadn't he sent a postcard? From somewhere up north? Lancashire? Yorkshire? What if it was Yorkshire? How near might she have been to him? But then Yorkshire was a huge county. He could be anywhere by now. He could be in Australia or America.

Gemma realised she'd come back home, in haste, with a half-formed hope that Kenny would be there. The chill of his absence had stayed with her. It had crept over her on the afternoon of the funeral. Its clammy cloak didn't leave her, even when Julie had arrived, smiling in her swirly kaftan and fancy boots, and so pleased to see her. Not even when the man with the very attractive voice had appeared at her door the next afternoon to invite her for a drink at the Still and West 'to sit and watch the ships coming in and out of the harbour and get to know each other a bit more'.

Sitting with Bruce in the pub, slowly sipping her glass of beer, she'd listened to the sound of his voice while staring out of the window at the rushing waters as the tide came in through the narrow harbour entrance. Turning towards Bruce when she felt his hand on her shoulder, she apologised for being distracted, excusing herself as tired after the travelling and the funeral. He'd had a slightly hurt look for a microsecond before this morphed into an eager smile as he stood, taking her arm by the elbow. He walked her back to Elizabeth's house. At the door he'd looked as if he'd like to kiss her, before lightly touching her cheek with a finger and saying goodnight.

The next morning, he was at the door again, inviting her to go for a walk up on the downs, as the weather had turned brighter. She'd felt unsure, but he was very persuasive, helped by Elizabeth telling her she was looking peaky and the fresh air would do her the world of good. Gemma had wondered if her mum was wanting her out of the house, maybe finding her presence beginning to irritate.

They had strolled through the tough grass on a path above one of the chalk pits on the side of Portsdown Hill and then sitting on a small blanket he'd brought (how thoughtful and kind), they'd looked at the view, and eaten a picnic of pork pies and fresh tomatoes with a triangle of cheese each, washed down with a bottle of ginger beer. Gemma realised she was relieved that they both had the horizon to look at as she'd been finding his direct gaze disconcerting.

For another week he'd sought Gemma out – to go on a day trip to the Isle of Wight, to go across to Hayling Island on the ferry to swim on a sandy beach, to go to see Cleopatra, the Richard Burton film that people were talking about. Puzzled at the contradiction between the delight of his voice and the discomfort of his gaze, Gemma was relieved when it was time to return to university. Then, when he asked her on the last evening if he could visit her up there sometime, telling her rather breathily that he thought she was 'so lovely and so special', she couldn't think of a reason to say no.

The Snow Queen's Palace

After his many months in Marit's world, each morning Kenny would slowly emerge from sleep to a consciousness of internal disarray. He would often have dreamed of Marit the gentle, Marit the kind, and also Marit the temptress, the siren, the bringer of enormous pleasure. But there would be dreams too of Marit the scold, the witch, the bully.

In the hours of darkness, she could still be the one with the warm hands, gently massaging his sore muscles after a long day of gardening. He could watch her beautiful face in the enormous mirror in front of the bath, seeing the concentration and, he thought, the pleasure on her face, while feeling her hands kneading and seeking out the knots in his back and neck. And on those glorious occasions when she had invited him to watch her step out of her silk dressing gown to join him in the scented warm water, his excitement had soared. All of this happened less frequently now, although the powerful memories of sensual pleasure didn't disappear, but rather lingered to leave him with anticipation and hope for these experiences to be repeated before too long. Sadly, Marit the angry Queen of Hearts (Off with his head!) was more often seen and heard these days and Kenny had to be increasingly alert to the small signals of her impending mood change. Her emotional weather could shift as quickly as a squall from nowhere at sea, but an experienced fisherman would know how to read the sky, and this is what he tried to do.

He first felt the ice-cold of her anger not very long after he'd arrived. Walking in the gardens on his own one day, he'd found himself looking at a bed full of lavender bushes, bees humming and thronging its network of twigs and flowers. They reminded him of the small lavender bush just outside Granny Sarah's back door. She would come into the little kitchen humming with pleasure when the flowers first appeared each summer and would pick just one or two sprigs that would live in a small vase until the flowers browned and fell around it in autumn. Thinking of his grandmother, Kenny had been stirred with regret that he hadn't said goodbye.

I should have let her know I'm OK.

Going out through a small side gate, he found himself running, not in fear but in a sudden burst of excitement as he realised how long it had been since he'd been driven in the dark into Marit's magical palace. And until now, feeling he was in heaven, why would he want to leave even for an hour?

In the village he found the small post office which sold postcards and stamps, and he quickly chose a view of the moors, purpled with heather, scattered with sheep and small stone houses, under an unnaturally blue sky. Kenny quickly wrote his message.

Dear Granny, Please don't worry about me. I am fine. I have
a good job as a gardener and am learning my trade. I am in a
great big place in Yorkshire. I will try and write again. Thank
you for all you have done for me. Love from your Kenny.

When he'd strolled back up the hill and found the gates locked, panic paralysed him. Had he fallen out of paradise, never to get back? And then there she was, Marit, looking at him through the bars of the gate, not speaking. With her eyes still on him, she unlocked the gate, and as it swung open, an icy voice he'd never heard from her before, told him to go inside. It was that evening when he first fully experienced being a possession. First understood that in this paradise, Marit's wishes were rules. Heaven was to come at a cost. Since that evening his heaven and hell had danced with each other till he felt dizzy. He never knew what to expect of the day or the night; kept an eye on himself with the hope of keeping heaven going for a bit longer; vigilant as a sailor about the sky and wind he would scan her facial expressions, or tones of voice for warning signs. Working out ways to please her.

There had been other times when he'd unwittingly broken a rule. A few days a month, the gardens were open to visitors, and she'd seen him talking on one of these days with a group of young students. He must have been showing too much eagerness to be in touch with people his own age when she saw him from a distance. The students couldn't have missed the sharpness of her voice calling for him to come into the house straight away.

After one of these darker moods, confusingly she could turn back to him with redoubled passion, leaving him feeling grateful and guilty for his anger towards her. And any ideas about trying to leave Marit's world would evaporate in the warmth of her eagerness for his body. But he recognised that each time Marit went away on one of her quests for antiques, he could feel peaceful and safe for a few glorious days.

It was hard to keep track of time. Had it been a year already? He had read about prisoners scratching marks on their cell wall to keep count of the days.

Marit had gone away very early this morning in her red car. It was high summer, and the gardens were overflowing with hollyhocks, roses, delphiniums, sunflowers, nasturtium and aubretia. He was trying to learn the names of all of the plants growing in the wide borders, with the help of regular instruction from Bert, who also supervised his usual tasks of weeding, watering and feeding the borders, and the heavier grind of the grass mowing. Pushing the lawnmower and roller had toughened the muscles in Kenny's now well-tanned arms. Marit seemed to be pleased at this and (in a good patch) she'd lie him down on his bed in the evening and rub his limbs and torso with some sweet-smelling Swedish oil which she said would nourish and preserve his youthful skin. These times with Marit the temptress could be intensely pleasurable, especially when she invited him to use the scented oil on her own soft skin… but he never knew when Marit the contemptuous would cruelly leave his side quite suddenly. Then he'd lie there in an invisible blanket of longing and shame.

The relief of her absence, when she went away for a few days, was palpable. Of course, she rarely told him how long she would be away, so the pleasure was always muted by uncertainty. Today, Kenny strolled along the now well-known paths and allowed his eyes to stray above the walls surrounding the gardens, towards the hills in the distance. He'd not been outside on his own since that first trip to post his card to Granny Sarah, but he'd travelled a little with Marit in the red car to other villages, where she had contacts with people in the antiques world. Sometimes she sold, sometimes she bought. She clearly had an expert eye for things and was a tough bargainer. He observed on these trips how people responded to her. Not, it seemed, with warm friendship, but more as a person to do business with. People were careful around her. He thought he caught the slight whiff of suspicion, even of undercurrents of dislike, but he dared not ask, after the first time. His simple questions that first day about what she felt about local people had caused that unpleasant narrowing of her eyes and tightening of her lips, and the drive back to the Hall was completed in an uncomfortable silence.

Wandering the paths on this hot afternoon, idly checking the state of the flowers, Kenny's mind was unusually free of the vigilance he'd acquired since arriving at Coldwater Hall. Again, he found lavender bushes nudging old images and feelings into the open space in his mind. And walking on further, suddenly, in a gap behind the shed, near Bert's spot for bonfires, a small patch of tall, pink-purple blooms of rosebay willowherb. Kenny's head swam for a moment, taking in the sight, the colour, the smell. Taken back to his childhood place of plays and stories – the remains of that bombed house in their street – willowherb thriving in cracks and corners. And Gemma, curly fair hair untidily falling over her forehead, Aertex shirt, shorts, plimsoles; Gemma smiling at him, bouncing the old soggy tennis ball against a still-standing wall.

In late August, with Marit away again, Kenny was mindlessly gathering weeds with one hand from the damp soil of the borders and stuffing them into the sack held in the other. Looking down at himself, Kenny saw the limbs of a grown man, a working man, muscled, tanned and very, very tired. How long had he been here? Slow steps took him to the pile of weeds behind the shed where a stand of now wispy, fading willowherb flowers still grew. Dropping the sack's contents onto the pile, Kenny picked a few inches from the top of the tall weed and held them to his face, shutting his eyes involuntarily to find again the bombsite, the street, the feeling of being known properly. But then, that time when he'd been invited to tea at Gemma's and she'd looked like a complete stranger and there'd been that man there with a silvery scar on one hand – the hand he'd been told to shake. He'd felt sure he'd lost his best friend but how good he'd felt when the old familiar Gemma came to his door after a few days, no longer with hair scraped into a strange shape by a ribbon. Where was she now? Always so clever, doing exams, probably some kind of student somewhere. And she and Elizabeth, always so kind to Granny Sarah. *Granny.* He should send her another card. He could take a chance while Marit was away and make a dash down the hill to the same little post office where he'd got the first card. He really should let her know where he is. And Gemma? Did she ever still think of him? That whole forgotten world – opening up in front of him as if—

'Kenny!'

He'd been daydreaming; hadn't heard the car or the gate. Marit was back and she was using her imperious voice. He felt his shoulders rise half an inch.

'What are you doing just standing there? I need you to help Desmond unload the car.'

(Desmond?)

Kenny walked over towards the red car, sprayed with mud, parked near the storeroom door at the back of the house.

Marit, dressed in a flowing Indian cotton garment, several rows of beads hanging in front of her visible and tanned breasts, was opening the boot and handing a wrapped oblong, maybe a picture frame, he thought, to a tall young man with shiny dark hair, which flopped over his eyes as he bent to take hold of the object. 'Thank you, Desmond, my sweet. Kenny, come and take this from me.' As Marit handed Kenny a stone statue, he nearly dropped it but staggered away from the car, aware of the sweet smell of that euphoria-inducing tobacco that she'd given him on his journey here. And he knew, with certainty that he should go.

On the Road

The decision to finally leave the prison of Marit's world had been sudden. Easy enough at that first impulsive moment, but soon watered down by doubts once he was out on a country road, in the chill of a damp dawn. Would he be followed? Would she perhaps be feeling regret? Might she be in tears at his departure, perhaps ashamed of her past treatment of him? Maybe if he went back now, took her a cup of her favourite coffee on a tray, with one of those late roses that she always told him she loved, in a small glass vase? She could be telling Desmond to go, right at this moment. Or would he be lying stretched out in her silky sheets, his skin smelling of her perfume? Had her long fair hair spilled over Desmond's face, hiding the intense pleasure on hers, in the night as it had for him so often. The sound of Kenny's angry footsteps echoed back to him from the stone walls either side of the narrow road. He momentarily imagined punching

Desmond hard, again and again. This thought propelled him on, and as his stride lengthened, his gardener's boots threw a rhythmic clanging up to him from the hard road, in time with the imagined fists.

Later, as the sun was just coming up, creeping into the sky over the curve of the early grey-green hillside, throwing into sharp relief the stone walls running across the fields, the extreme beauty of the dales and the freedom of being out, being his own person, being out of her view, held him to his decision, taking him further and further away from Coldwater Hall.

The grinding gears of a lorry, reaching him across the low, misted fields, told him he was nearing the main road to Richmond. Spotting a stone block next to a gateway, he sat, and putting down his old school rucksack, unwrapped the food he'd filched from the kitchen after supper, late the previous evening. He'd helped, as he often did, with the clearing of the table, leaving Marit to her new guest, and then he'd wandered out onto the terrace for a smoke. Through the uncurtained window he'd watched them for a moment. The sight of Desmond's face, entranced by Marit's attentions, as his had been, more than a year ago, brought everything into sharp focus. He was looking through a clear window at himself. Seeing Marit's dance of heaven and hell as just that. A dance. A dance of a puppeteer with her toy on strings. How often in the last year had he struggled with an urge to run away? How often had she drawn him back, with the sudden intimacy that her unexpected nearness could create? The hand on the back of his neck, and the subtle smell of her skin as she'd stroked his forehead, brushing his hair back before placing her lips on his.

As the sun rose higher in the sky, he ate the bread, cheese and left-over pie. As the flavours reached his taste buds, he watched a vivid red admiral's quick movements as it danced from flower to purple flower. As if in tune with the butterfly, an image fluttered, of running after a ball, chasing it, catching it, throwing it, seeing the ball caught. Seeing a smile. Feeling his own smile. He thought, I'm going in the right direction.

Once onto the main road, he started to stick out his thumb each time he heard a grumbling engine coming up behind him. After an hour, which felt like a day, he recognised the sound of an engine slowing, gears changing, brakes grinding.

'Where you wanting, laddie?' The face under the flat cap was smiling down from the cab through the opened door.

'Not sure, but I want to get down south,' Kenny said, stretching his head up and back to meet the face, 'so maybe anywhere in the London direction?'

'London eh? Well, I can't get you all the way there, but will Richmond do? Hop in and I'll drop you in the transport café. You'll pick up another lift for sure from there.'

The first driver had treated him to a cup of dark brown tea and an iced bun. Then he'd found another driver who was going on as far as Darlington. This one kept asking questions, almost as if he knew Kenny was escaping from something. What could he say? He tried talking about the gardening, trying to deflect the man's curiosity.

'I'd been there a while and to tell the truth I was getting bored with gardening. I'm fed up with the countryside. I fancy a go at the big city.'

'You sure? Wouldn't do for me. It's all noise and fuss and to-do down there. Got a sister down in London, me. I can't get away quick enough when I've been to see her. Lord, the smell of the air is thick as Guinness, and the traffic, and there's all sorts of folk down there... Well, you'll find out soon enough.'

'Well, it will be a change from up in the dales with just sheep to talk to.'

'What about your boss up there? Did he treat you OK? You've not been given yer cards, have you?'

Kenny could feel his heart beating faster as the man's question stirred an image of "his boss". Marit in the huge wall mirror soaping his back in the bath; Marit frowning at him through the gates when he'd gone down to the village without asking. It took him a moment to answer.

'No, my choice to come away. He was OK, I suppose. A bit moody, bossy like most bosses. It was hard to always get things right. It was time for a change anyway.' His uninteresting answers soon discouraged more questions and instead Kenny had to listen to a monologue about the man's family, the mean bosses he'd had, journeys he'd made, breakdowns he'd had to deal with, the stupidity of the minister of transport. By the time they were in the outskirts of Darlington, Kenny was relieved to be able to get down from the cab, which had smelled strongly of the driver's roll-up cigarettes and his unwashed trousers.

Hour after hour. Lift after lift. Hours waiting between lifts, Drivers who were gruff, drivers who were too friendly, drivers who never spoke, drivers who never shut up. As day turned to night, Kenny drifted in and out of sleep as he reversed his journey with Marit the year before – now from north to south. Roll-ups this time and cold tea from a thermos rather than Marit's sweet-smelling cigarettes that had made everything look and sound so beautiful, and sips from her silver brandy flask. No soft woollen blanket to keep him warm, and no scent of spice and musk.

Once past Birmingham, the road became wider, noisier, full of lights; white lights coming up behind, red in front, flashing lights as vehicles roared past in the next lane. It was hard to sleep but also hard to stay fully awake. A bitter coffee woke him up at a huge roadside café stop, a place full of exhausted-looking drivers, where he changed lorries for the last time and found a driver who offered to take him right into London.

Who Am I?

By the time Gemma travelled back to the Yorkshire pub from her lodgings in Birmingham to retrieve her walking boots and gear, it was autumn and the light of late summer was all but gone. Beryl had seemed put out, had done her sniffing thing loudly and had offered dark warnings about the dangers of the moors at this time of the year.

'You can't ever rely on the weather up there, y'know. The clocks go back in a couple of weeks. And mind you don't go missing too many lectures.'

'Beryl, I promise I'll be very careful. And I'll phone from the village when I'm about to leave. Don't go letting my room to anyone else!'

Dried leaves blew on and off the bus window and the hillside heather was losing its purple glow as she was carried up the dale to the village where she'd felt so warmly welcomed in

August. She hadn't let Bruce know where she was going and felt a small pang of anxiety, mixed with a frisson of disloyalty and freedom. Why did he always want to know everything?

Gemma found the old pub empty except for a couple of local farmers propping up the bar, involved in conversation about sheep dipping. She sat alone in the same corner where she'd been in the summer with the noisy, lively group of hikers. Feeling invisible now, she was glad when the waitress came to bring her the pie and chips. Although it was a different, rather impatient girl from the friendly one in the summer, Gemma wanted to keep her talking, suddenly really needed to feel someone's gaze. *If no one sees me, am I really here?* When she was still little, she always knew she was there because Elizabeth, Mrs Crawley or Kenny could see her, they knew she was there.

After her meal, she walked out into the darkness of the village square to the red phone box and called Bruce.

Gemma had breakfast in the empty bar next morning, after a restless night. She'd felt so alone and had wanted the comfort of hearing Bruce's voice, but as soon as she'd told him where she was, his tone had changed. Why had she gone away without letting him know? He had been worried. Didn't she know how fond of her he was? He wanted to always keep her safe. He could have arranged to come with her. Maybe she hadn't wanted him with her. Maybe there was someone in the village who... And so it went on, with Gemma finding herself over-explaining, over-reassuring, swearing that of course there was no one else. Walking back in the dark to the pub, Gemma wondered why she'd agreed to Bruce joining her here for a few days. Well, at least he wouldn't be here until tomorrow. She could go for a long walk and clear her head a bit. Perhaps she'd misunderstood him – even been unkind. It was, as he'd said, only that he cared for her. He'd only been offering his support.

Over a breakfast of local sausages, well-poached eggs, toast and marmalade, she examined her thoughts, trying to tease out the layers of discomfort. Bruce had made her feel important, had given her a sense of being valued, thought about, kept in mind. But was that more the kind of thing you might get from a caring but stern father? Maybe this was what had always been missing and she hadn't realised it, or named it, until now. Sipping the half-cold coffee, she tried to remember Donald, her dad. When he'd turned up, out of the blue, smelling of pipe smoke and hair cream, and with that horrid scar on his hand, she'd wanted to be pleased, but it had felt stiff and awkward. Everyone was supposed to be over the moon. Husbands and wives joyfully reunited, children and fathers affectionately meeting, sometimes for the first time.

Her mother had insisted on putting her into her best frock, which she hated, had made her hair all different after the torture of the Maison Pearson spiky brush. The final straw was the addition of a stupid big ribbon. Elizabeth had scrubbed her nails with a nailbrush so hard that it had hurt. She felt like someone else. She felt all "Not Gemma". Like Alice in Wonderland when she'd fallen down the hole. (Alice had wondered if she was someone else, as everything was so confusing. Maybe she was Mabel. 'Tell me who I am and then I'll come up,' Alice had said out loud.) Gemma had wondered about all that saying thoughts out loud in the book, because in real life people were called mad or very old if they did that. When Kenny and Granny Sarah came for tea that day to meet her dad, she could tell that Kenny didn't like how she looked, because he'd turned his back on her. Maybe he wondered if she was Mabel!

And then a strange thought. Did Bruce know she was Gemma? It sometimes felt as if she was always having to live up to a different Gemma in his head.

In the afternoon, she set off, armed with a local map from the little post office, feet well-laced up again in her walking boots, and muffled up with her university scarf. She followed the signs to the riverside path which she knew went all the way to the next village. In the summer she'd walked it, loving the meadow flowers, brushing off hazes of insects, sheep calling each other in the distance. Now the ground was claggier underfoot, the meadows were duller, but she could still hear the call of birds, the bleating of sheep – was still enjoying it. But tomorrow, would it be better or worse to be walking with Bruce?

When Gemma reached the old stone humpback bridge over the river, she went to stand on the highest part of the stone curve to look down into the iron-brown water. Silence, but for the water flowing below her, the rustle of invisible birds in the trees nearby, and the background muffled stumbling of distant sheep. She became aware of her feet and their contact with the ground, and the feather touch of the slight breeze on her cheeks. Memories of childhood games of Pooh-sticks played with Kenny on a little bridge in the park on their way home from school.

Footsteps? An old man in country clothes was coming towards her. Cloth cap that looked as if it had grown to fit his head exactly, muddy boots probably of the same vintage, clothes of some kind of dark-greenish beige palette. He was walking slowly and puffing a bit as he reached the curved stone side of the bridge next to her.

'Where you off to, lass? You'll not be from round these parts?'
'Hello there. No, I'm from down south. Just visiting.'

'You on your way to somewhere or staying round here? It'll be dark afore too long. Don't want to get yourself lost. I never gets lost, me, 'cos I been here since I were a nipper, you see. You gets to see in the dark then.'

'Thanks, but I'm ready to turn round and go back to where I'm staying. The Bull's Head. You know it?'

'Know it, good Lord. If I could have a halfpenny for every pint of Theakston's Old Peculiar I've drunk there, I'd be rich. So, are you here for long or just flying in, like?'

'A few more days. My boyfriend comes here tomorrow so I need to show him around. I don't know if he's much of a walker so I thought maybe a bus trip somewhere nice to have tea and cake. Any recommendations on where to go?'

The man's hand went to find his chin and explored the feel of it for a while, as he leaned his other arm on the bridge and looked down into the water.

'Well, depends what you'd be after. You could do worse than walk on up to the next village and get yourself an early supper at the Kestrel, but then you'd be best walking back to your Bull's Head along the road in the dark. But then again, there are one or two places with big old houses, gardens, tea rooms, that kind of thing. You could try one of those by bus if you check the timetable by the bus stop first. There's the Ghyll – that's about five mile away, I reckon, and then there's that Coldwater Hall, but that'd be a bit further on. No tea and cake, but wonderful gardens. And there's a teashop in the village. Nobody takes to 'er that owns it, mind. Stuck-up sort of woman, she is. But nice enough grounds to walk about in, from what I hear. Depends a bit what you're after doing.'

Like a thin drift of smoke, a picture from her last summer night at the pub flitted into her mind and out again; a foreign woman who'd bought a big place with cash, who wasn't liked, who had handsome young gardeners. She realised the man was looking at her waiting for some response, and she quickly smiled and thanked him.

'I'd better set off back. Don't want to get caught in the dark as I'm not born and bred here.'

They both smiled and she wanted to hug him, not knowing quite why.

In spite of looking forward to seeing Bruce, Gemma wondered why his eagerness when he arrived made her want to take a step back.

What was wrong with her?

She went to meet him the following afternoon in Richmond. He'd thrown his arms around her and kissed her right there at the bus station and she'd shrunk back a bit in embarrassment, but then they'd got on board and settled themselves into the little bus for the journey up the dale and she felt pleased to have him sitting next to her. Until he started asking her all the usual questions. How was she? What had she been doing? Had any of the people she'd told him about, that she'd met in the summer, been around?

Whenever Bruce did this, Gemma had an urge to hold some small unimportant details tight inside, not that the details were in any way private, but she didn't want to feel her head being scoured out of its contents. She didn't see why she should always have to account for movements and thoughts all the time. Then she would scold herself, telling herself that it was natural for him to be asking – he was her boyfriend, he cared, he was interested. Maybe it was something in her that was missing.

When the little bus arrived in the centre of the village, they walked over to the pub. She'd booked him a separate room for the next two nights. When she took him up to show him where he'd be sleeping, Bruce turned to her as soon as they were inside the room, clasping her close, until she felt slightly suffocated by the roughness of his tweed jacket. He sensed her slight pull away from him.

'What's the matter, sweetheart? You haven't gone all frigid on me, have you? I've been longing to touch you, imagining it all the way up from London.'

'Sorry, no, of course not, Bruce. It was just your jacket tickling me. I didn't want to sneeze over your lovely new jacket.'

And inside her head she asked herself why she always had to make up things. Why not say she didn't particularly like the new jacket? And no, she didn't feel ready for a passionate embrace, she needed to take her time, and his eager expectations of her made her cross and when she felt cross with him, she couldn't fancy him, but she was sure she would fancy him again if they could just go downstairs and have pie and chips and a glass of beer. And she was sorry to be such a disappointment and of course it was all her fault.

Although Bruce had been persuasive, they hadn't had proper full sex yet. She'd told herself that she'd seen too many girls fall pregnant, after being assured by boyfriends they were 'taking care of things and it would all be quite safe'. She'd had a few brief carnal moments in her first year away from home, before she'd met Bruce. But these had felt playful and relaxed in their momentariness and had never got quite as far as risking pregnancy. She knew she could feel excitement and pleasure, but somehow with Bruce, well, the more he tried to insist, the more she drew back. She so wanted to be in a proper relationship, and she kept hoping she would feel she was, and then maybe she'd get better at the whole business. She didn't want to *not* please him. But she wished they could go back to the kissing and holding hands of the late summer for a while, and then slowly work up to things. He'd been much too quick to say he loved her, to say he wanted her, to ask her to reciprocate with the same enthusiasm. When he'd visited her in Birmingham, he'd seemed suddenly to expect so much of her, away from Southsea. And then to be so cross and even critical of her for making him so miserable, and after he'd made the effort to come all that way to see her. And didn't she know how she made him feel?

Downstairs in the bar they ordered food and drinks and she told him of her plans for the next day.

'There's a bus we can take to a really big place a few miles away with gorgeous gardens, and they say there's a tea shop in the village with lovely home-made cakes.'

'But I thought we could maybe go for a long country walk and take a picnic. Like we did in the summer on Portsdown Hill. Remember? That's where I first kissed you.'

'Of course, I remember. And we had a delicious picnic of pork pie and ginger beer, and it was so clear we could see for miles and miles, way past the Isle of Wight.'

'You were looking out to sea, and I was just looking at you. I think that was when I was sure I was falling in love with you. That's why I've been travelling halfway round the country to see you. So do let me choose what we do tomorrow. And this place you want to visit, we could go the next day.'

'OK Bruce, let's do that. But the house and gardens do sound magnificent. I met someone on my walk, a local chap, who recommended it.'

Gemma sensed Bruce stiffening slightly and turning to her. Scanning her face in that way of his.

'What sort of a local chap, sweetheart? Was he chatting you up? Or maybe you were chatting him up?'

Gemma found it hard to sleep that night, knowing that Bruce was in the next room. Every time she woke, and opened her eyes, the thin curtained window stared back at her, stirring discomforting images. When Bruce had ordered their evening meal in the bar, he had bought her more wine than she wanted, more than she was used to drinking, and she'd felt a little light-headed as they went up the creaking wooden stairs. Bruce had said he'd like to tuck her in and had followed her into her room. Gemma had pleaded tiredness, but he was clearly hoping the wine might have made her more amenable. He started to kiss her, but then his hands were roaming around her back and then her front until she couldn't bear it and said 'No' quite loudly, surprising herself and him.

He looked up at her, upset and even a trifle cross.

'Why, sweetheart? Why not? You have let me before, and I seem to remember you enjoying my touching you there.'

And this was true. And he could see that she knew it was true, and his hand moved slowly back to gently search for a nipple under the pink jumper. And he kissed her again and this time she felt the relief of allowing herself to feel pleasure, relief too at being able to please him. She wanted to be like other people. To be in a relationship, to have a boyfriend, and if she couldn't please him, he'd hate her and disappear and she'd be alone and she'd always have that dreadful feeling of invisibility.

Things had continued, lying together on the bed, until the

moment when she had to say nothing and let things carry on, or say please stop. And she had said, "Please stop now, Bruce." She'd tried to say it nicely, in a soft and affectionate way, in a way that suggested that maybe it was no, but just for now, not for ever. And he'd climbed off the bed, bent to kiss her cheek, before walking to the door with a rather theatrical sigh.

After breakfast, Gemma collected the packed lunch from the kitchen. Standing just outside the pub door they bent to get their walking boots laced, and with waterproof jackets zipped up, they set off on the path from the village. Squeezing through the gap in the first stone wall they found the marked path. After a rather wet October, the field was soggy and dented with hoof marks and cow pats, but there were large flagstones at intervals creating the path down to the riverside. Reaching the small wooden bridge, they crossed over to pick up the route that she was now familiar with.

As the sun emerged, Gemma began to enjoy the day, and to feel more comfortable about what had gone on the previous evening. Maybe she just needed time, needed not to be rushed into things and everything would work out. She wanted to feel normal, didn't want to feel cross, or be thought frigid.

'Is there someone else you aren't telling me about, Gemma?'

Turning to look at Bruce, she recognised his expression. She'd seen it a few times. Always excused him as being just insecure, as feeling so much for her he couldn't bear to have doubts. Understood that he might worry about her when they were apart.

'Why do you say that, Bruce? You know there isn't.'

'Oh, just a feeling, you know. You seem to be able to relax OK with other people. Those students you met here, the man you met on your walk. Maybe I'm a fool and being led a dance by you. Maybe you like being touched well enough but don't want to commit to someone. In it for the fun and laughs but nothing more. Is that it?'

His voice was rising in tone and in volume, and she couldn't bear it.

'No, Bruce. Stop this nonsense, for heaven's sake. There isn't anyone else.'

Gemma walked quickly on, ducking under the damp overhanging branches, watching her feet carefully where mud and stones risked a slip. She went on for a while without looking back to see if he was following her. Then hearing him some way behind, she slowed her pace, thinking it better not to annoy him further. When he caught up with her, his expression was different. Regretful, anxious, almost pleading.

'Darling, I'm sorry. Forgive me. You know it's because I've never felt like this about anyone before. You walked into my life at that old lady's funeral and you've been in my head every minute since. Please let's have a lovely day, a wonderful picnic and I promise I'll behave. Show me your favourite walk and tomorrow we'll go to this grand palace and gardens you've been on about.'

With peace restored, they went on along the narrow path until, coming out of the trees, it rejoined the riverside. The views ahead opened up and the walking got easier. For a while they could stride next to each other and Bruce took her hand gently. They exchanged a few observations as they walked: the brown of the water, the occasional flit of an unknown bird. When the nearby silly sheep voices made them both smile, Gemma began to feel that things were really fine and she'd worried too much. Reaching the humpback bridge, Gemma wanted to stand again on the top of its small hill and stare at the water in the silence, to drink in the tranquillity before they settled down on a large stone seat for their picnic. But Bruce was talking at her and she was finding his voice grating. It was, she had often thought, as if he had two completely separate voice boxes, producing from one the rich deep sound which could leave her feeling stroked and calmed and even sometimes excited, a friendly voice, reassuring and comforting, a voice she missed when she didn't hear it, a voice that made her feel safe and sheltered. His other voice had a harsh edge to it, and the words came faster, revving up as if ready to strike – an unnerving voice that sought answers, spat accusations. She felt as if this voice was robbing her now of her new favourite place. And she realised he was using this voice to ask her about the postcard.

'And what's this?'

Kenny's postcard, which she'd slipped into a side pocket of her rucksack before leaving her mother's house. She'd forgotten it was there. The card, with its vivid blue sky, purple heather and sheep had been sitting on Elizabeth's mantlepiece in the kitchen, and just on an impulse Gemma had taken it.

'Oh, I'd forgotten I'd put it in the rucksack. It was when I was home at Mum's.'

'Kenny! It says Kenny! I thought you said he'd not been heard of for years.'

'Well, yes. But Mum showed me this card when I was home. She'd found it at Sarah Crawley's when she was cleaning out the place. You knew she was doing that. You were there.'

'So why did you take it? A card from an old schoolfriend? Or maybe something more?'

'Bruce, that's ridiculous. You're being ridiculous. Kenny was, and is, someone I've known as long as I can remember. He was never a boyfriend.'

'Strange then that you had to take this card and keep it close to you. Maybe I don't know you at all, Gemma.'

111

'Maybe you don't!' she heard herself say under her breath.

His voice was higher now, louder, his words like bullets aimed at her. She wanted him to stop, but in that moment thought, I can't bear this, but it will stop if I apologise, if I give in, if I just try to please him. Otherwise, he will get angrier and angrier.

And just at that moment it started to rain very heavily.

Back in the pub, drenched and shivering, Gemma asked the young guy behind the bar for a brandy. Bruce had rushed up to his room to get dry and change, thinking she was following as soon as she'd booked them in for dinner. But she didn't follow him. Instead, she sat on a bar stool. Shivering. The brandy was for her nerves as much as her cold.

'Coming down stair rods, the rain now, my love.'

'Certainly is.'

'You want to be getting those wet clothes off quick, if you ask me,' he said with a big smile and a wink just as Bruce came through the door into the bar.

Gemma heard the door open and looked back. Bruce was pale. He came over and sat on the bar stool next to her without a word. She wasn't fooled by his silence. In the few months they'd been seeing each other, she'd become alert to changes in his expression. Of face and voice. And without a doubt, he was furious. It would only be a matter of time before he'd tell her why, not that she couldn't guess. Sitting on a bar stool, soaking wet, having a drink with a handsome, winking barman. Even if Bruce hadn't heard the whole conversation about how she should "get her wet clothes off quick".

She was eating breakfast alone the next morning after seeing Bruce off on the bus. They'd said little. He'd tried the 'I'm so sorry, darling. I was out of order. It will not happen again. It's just that you are so important to me' stuff, but for once she'd stood her ground. The night before had been ghastly and everyone in the pub must have heard the shouting. And the thump when she fell against the bed post after he'd pushed her, and she had cried out in pain. When someone did come and knock on the door to ask if everything was all right, she took the opportunity to slip out of his room and go into hers, quickly locking the door with shaking hands. He'd come and tried the door, and then knocked of course. And cried. Sobbed like a child. And knocked again harder. And swore at her. And went back to his room. In the morning, an exhausted and dry-eyed Gemma went downstairs and waited for him. And told him he should go.

It was like waking from a dream. Sitting over her cold scrambled eggs and toast, her eyes looking blankly into thin air through the shaft of dust-moted sunlight coming through the window. Her mind roamed over the previous months, remembering how she'd welcomed Bruce's attentions: his strokes, his cuddles and his admiration. Then she remembered all his baseless accusations and interrogations. As time went on, he'd suspected her, sneered, sworn at her as if he was seeing a completely different Gemma from who she thought was. And there'd been times when she'd almost believed that he was right. It had come at her in letters, cards, phone calls – even when he wasn't actually with her. Now he was gone, but would she have the strength to keep him away? She feared being alone and cold, dreaded the sense of invisibility, the feeling of a terrible smallness she could have, like Alice when she shrank and fell into the pool of tears, she thought. Leaving her uneaten breakfast, she went up to her room and got into bed, pulling the covers almost over her head and she slept. She slept for most of the day, coming downstairs briefly for something to eat and another brandy before going back under the covers like a sick cat seeking a warm place to curl up in.

When Gemma opened her eyes next morning, it was a moment before she remembered. Bruce. Had he really gone? You can be afraid of someone without knowing you are afraid until they have gone. Looking at her watch, she leapt out of bed. Throwing on her jeans and jumper, she grabbed the rucksack, jacket and purse and headed off downstairs, grabbing a coffee and a piece of toast before dashing out to catch the bus. Sitting in the bus, she took out Kenny's postcard, now slightly torn. She'd made a grab for it and snatched it from Bruce's hand. Turning it over, back to front to back, she wished it could speak. He'd written it. Where? He'd posted it. Where? The franking mark on the stamp was too indistinct. No clues there. The picture was too generic. No place name. Just a view of the dales. But what if it was Coldwater Hall? Surely not. But an image arose of a tall blonde woman standing by a red car, her hand reaching up to stroke a young man's face. Stop being so stupid, she told herself and stuffed the card back in the side pocket.

Without Bruce beside her, her thoughts were swinging between fear of the future and an exciting sense of freedom. Perhaps she should have just headed back to Birmingham. Safety in numbers there. And she could change her lodgings – move into a shared place with some of the girls in her year. Maybe she needn't worry so much and Bruce would accept that it was over.

Changing buses in the next village, she began to worry that she'd made a mistake. The driver's voice cut through her day-dreaming to tell her this was her stop. As she got off, she checked the time of the return bus and asked which way she should walk for Coldwater Hall. The village was small but very pretty, with just one grocery shop, doubling as a post office. A tiny cottage next door had a sign in a window saying "Hot Drinks and Cakes", but another sign on the front door said "Closed". Gemma set off up the lane. After stopping to get her breath and retie her boot laces, she looked up and caught sight of the Hall behind its high stone walls. Taking a look back at where she'd climbed, the glorious view took her breath away again. Reaching the large iron entrance gates to the grounds, she read the information board that confirmed what she'd been told. Today was one of the open days for visitors to the gardens. And then, didn't Alice see a beautiful garden through a door but she was too big to get through and wished she could shut up like a telescope?

As she stood, hesitantly, an old man pushing a wheelbarrow full of prunings came past the gate and said, 'It's OK, my love. It's open, and you just put your money in that little money box over there. Gardens is open but not the house, OK?' And then, rather curiously he added, 'You're all right. Madam is away this afternoon.'

Gemma was soon strolling round the herbaceous borders, which were still magnificent in spite of the lateness of the season. And with the backdrop of the moors, she wished she'd got a camera. She started imaginary conversations with her mum about what she was seeing, was swayed by a sudden burst of homesickness, wondered what it would be like to tell her mother about Bruce. She'd ring home and promise she'd be back as soon as term was over and stay the whole of the Christmas vacation.

The place was very quiet as she explored. She was pleased when, around a corner, the old man appeared again, now with an empty barrow and a pipe smouldering in the corner of his mouth.

'You'm looking cold, my love. Don't you go stopping too long.'

'Good idea. It's getting chilly. But it's been lovely being here. The gardens must be stunning in the summer. Pretty good even now. I actually quite like all those tall faded ones there. What are they?'

'Chrysanthemums mostly and some Echinacea just at back of 'em.'

'What a lot of work it must be for you. Have you worked here a long time?'

'A good bit of time, aye. Worked for the old family before Madam arrived.' He took a long pull on the pipe, coughed a little before going on. 'But no, too much for me all on my own. Madam usually has apprentices, young lads here, and it's my job to train them up. But she gets bored with 'em after a while.' While he continued, sucking noisily on his pipe, Gemma was struggling to frame a question, but the old man went on, 'New one here now, knows nowt about gardening yet, but I'll do my best. Last one 'ere had quite a talent for it, but he headed off one night in late August when we were all sleeping, so my work is cut out now trying to shape this new one up. He's off out with her now, buying old country stuff to do up and sell on.' He had an unreadable expression for a moment, looked about him and then down at his boots and gave another small cough. 'You go on now, lass. It gets dark soon enough this time of year and you'll not be wanting to miss your bus.'

Part Four

Is Anyone There?

It was an old Victorian house with draughty windows and a slightly uneven wooden floor, but only five minutes from the park, with its ducks and swans and plenty of space to walk. Beryl, her first landlady, was sad at her departure. She had always seemed to need Gemma's presence more than Gemma had needed the roof over her head. It had been OK in many ways, but the row with Bruce had been the spur for her to make a move.

Gemma had found two other girls from the university to share with her and, after settling on this place, they had all gone shopping one blustery, sunny Saturday afternoon to the Bullring Market and come back to the house with multicoloured pieces of Indian material from a stall to throw over the lumpy old chairs and beds. The odds and ends of cheap and chunky blue and white china they'd picked up looked absolutely fine on the

119

shelves of the tiny kitchen they shared so it was starting to feel quite like home. Gemma liked the company of Imogen and Ruth. Glad to be somewhere new.

She didn't know how Bruce had found out her new address, but he had, appearing at the door one Sunday morning in mid-November, a month after the massive row in the Yorkshire pub, the weekend she'd finally had enough of his suffocating attentions, his constant questioning of her movements, of his unwarranted suspicions about her loyalty. Then, in spite of his tearful pleading, apologies and protestations of love, she had told him to go away and leave her alone, and he'd gone.

His reappearance caught her at a low moment. Ruth and Imogen were both off visiting family for the weekend and she'd decided to stay in the flat and get some coursework done in peace and quiet. But peace and quiet had quickly turned to oppressive silence and then that familiar and frightening feeling of emptiness, of invisibility, that she hated. No one could see her, no one could hear her voice except herself (and finding herself talking to the steamed-up bathroom mirror for a moment after a bath had made her feel a bit mad). Walking through to put the kettle on, she heard her footsteps, but they seemed to not belong to her. So how was she to know she existed?

On Sunday morning, after a restless night full of dreams, she woke and went down in her dressing gown to put the kettle on. Surprised to hear the knock on the door, she opened it to find Bruce on the doorstep, carrying a small rucksack, a bottle of red wine and a huge bunch of roses.

The kettle was already humming, so somewhat warily she felt she should ask him in. Heart thumping, she went into the kitchen and made them both some Nescafé in two of the new blue and white mugs. Looking at her own slightly shaking hands spooning in the coffee, pouring the hot water, stirring in the milk, and then pushing the prickly rose stems into a jam jar of water, she tried to gather her shaken thoughts. After a quick squint in the kitchen mirror, she pulled the belt of her old dressing gown a bit tighter before going back into the sitting room with the coffee and the flowers.

She found Bruce already settled in an armchair. A turbulence of fear, and anxious pleasure, struggled within her, and so she sat in the other armchair and listened as he told her, in several different ways, how sorry he'd been about their awful last meeting. He'd been out of order, completely to blame. He absolutely understood how his suspicions had hurt her. It was just that he felt such overwhelming affection for her, such love. She had no idea how miserable he had been without her. After weeks of torment, he could now understand his own and her feelings properly... And so on. His blue eyes watered as he spoke. He even cried real tears – put his hands over his face – lowered his head to his knees in his distress.

Gemma instinctively put out a sympathetic hand to touch his shoulder, and he grasped it, catching it up to meet his lips and she found his touch warmed her and she began to wonder if she'd been the one who was in the wrong when she'd sent him packing. After the destabilising loneliness of this solitary weekend, it was easy for her to find herself remembering the warmth of his admiration, the feeling of belonging when she'd been held and thought about by Bruce. He'd made her feel real and known, and she'd missed that. Any recall of the difficulties – his intrusiveness, the obsessiveness of his attachment to her – she pushed to the back of her mind, telling herself that they were things to work on in the future. All couples have difficulties which need to be sorted out, don't they? It wasn't his fault that she'd slipped in the middle of that horrible shouting match, and banged into the bedpost. And the bruises had soon faded.

And so, she let him stay. And by late Sunday night, when Ruth and Imogen came back, it seemed that he and she were again a couple. And by this time, she had allowed Bruce into her bed.

The Streets of London

Kenny knew what month it was, but it was hard to keep track of the date. He listened to the rush of shoppers each day, and after dark noticed the increase in numbers of raucous young people smelling of alcohol who would stagger past without seeing him. He felt invisible. He was certain he was invisible. Sometimes one would vomit or urinate against a wall near him, and his nostrils would fill with the stench, and his belly with anger. He was getting used to that now. What he couldn't get used to was the cold. It had been light till quite late when he'd first arrived in the city. The warmth of an early September day had lasted well into the evening. Finding a deckchair to sleep in in Hyde Park had been easy enough. But by early October the night chill had driven him into the warmer streets of the West End. Now, he woke each morning stiff with cold, in spite of the torn sleeping bag he had found in an alley, and stayed cold, arms holding each elbow close to his ribs, unless he was able to grab a doorway to a heated office block or department store, or find a ventilation grill blowing out warm air.

Kenny had seen in an old newspaper that the clocks had gone back, so knew it was at least towards the end of October. Now darkness fell by late afternoon, although Oxford Street was brightly lit. A few Christmas trees were already appearing in the bigger shop windows, sharing the spaces with blind models in party clothes, giant teddy bears, and Father Christmases grasping improbable pretend parcels. Why did the first signs of Christmas appear even before Bonfire Night? He knew that must be close because of the occasional bang of fireworks being let off in side streets at night. And then you couldn't miss the odd trussed-up figure lying slumped in a battered pram next to a plate, a piece of cardboard propped up, saying, "Penny for the Guy". More reminders of his childhood.

One year, he and Gemma had eagerly screwed up newspaper to stuff into one of Granny Sarah's jumpers and a pair of a neighbour's torn trousers. They'd been allowed to sit at the corner of their street, with the Guy perched on Gemma's old doll's pram, and had collected enough coins to buy a couple of Catherine wheels and golden rain from the corner shop. Mrs Siddons had insisted they wear gloves the next evening when the sparklers were passed round by the bonfire in Mr and Mrs Hodges's back garden next door. When their wonderful guy met its end in a glorious conflagration, they were both fascinated and shocked.

Often, of an evening now, Kenny would be standing near to the light and heat emanating from one of the posher shops, his hand held out to passers-by, hoping for enough coins to cover the cost not of a Catherine wheel but of a sandwich or bag of chips.

*

Kenny's eyes are shut, but he isn't fully asleep. A built-in vigilance is now well established. Ears always half-tuned to footsteps, the pace of them, the kind of shoe and to the wearer's stride. In this, his newest resting place under an arch near Waterloo Station, it is even easier to judge. He prefers it here away from the shops and bars – safer than the West End anyway. That last kicking from a drunk, on Bonfire Night, had sent him here, near to the river, away from the crowds. It is easier here, under the echoing stonework, to interpret any approaches – can tell pretty well by the sounds: the scuff of cheap trainers with laces dangling, the clack of polished well-heeled brogues, the small, teetering steps of girls with tall, spike-heeled boots, the aggressive clunk of Doc Martens. But he can't always tell who might slow down just enough to put a few coins in his hat, with a quiet 'there ye'are, mate', who will walk on past, or who will silently stoop down to pop a sausage roll or ham sandwich by his side, or who will slow their pace just enough to raise his hopes before offering him a gobby spit or a kick and a curse.

If he does fall fully asleep, he will often dream. Sometimes he is on the seafront at Southsea, listening to the waves, happy and safe in the old shelter, until he hears the fearful screams as he is dragged by an irresistible current under the water. If he dreams of Marit, he will wake up either with clenched angry fists, or in a haze of physical desire. She remains a jigsaw of mismatched pieces still, whether he is asleep or awake. Frequent replays of conversations with her spin in his mind when he is conscious. Fragments of these circulate in a dance in his head, every time his eyes shut.

'You see, I was always my father's favourite, Kenny.

He would tell me how boring my mother was. He'd say she lacked passion.

He said the worst thing I could do was to be boring. I was never to be afraid of passion, he'd tell me.

And I should always seek beautiful things and beautiful people.

He told me that people should decide what they want and then make sure they get it.'

She'd also said, one night when she seemed to feel closer to him in mind as well as body, 'He always told me how beautiful I was. I went everywhere with him and then one day he just died.'

That time he remembered so well. It was the only time he ever saw a tear in her eye.

These thoughts are interrupted now by footsteps approaching. Strong shoes, good shoes, confident stride, slight smell of a cigar.

Slowing.

Stopping.

Stronger smell of cigar.

Slight hint of expensive aftershave.

'Good evening, young sir. You look a little cold and also a tiny bit fed up. Yes?'

Kenny sits up straighter and tries to focus on the face above him. It is in shadow, although the expensive shoes are catching light from a small roof lamp. 'So you are here why, young sir?'

'What? Why do you think?'

'You don't smell of the beer or the cider, and you are not pretending you can play a guitar or sing. Did you once have a job? Did you have place to live?'

Kenny doesn't know how to answer. Doesn't know why the man is asking.

'So, please to tell me, what is it that you can do?'

'Sorry, what? Yes. I mean I don't know. Yes, I was working.

126

Up north. Gardening and things.' Kenny is struggling to get up on his feet, but he's been sitting for so long he staggers a bit.

'And now you are here. Not so very many gardens round here, I don't suppose!' He smiles, as if pleased with his small joke. 'And tell me, what else can you do for a kind of job?'

Kenny thinks the man isn't English, although he speaks well enough. There is just something about the way he uses words. It was like that with Marit. She had a way of using familiar words but in a slightly different way. But this man doesn't sound like her. So probably not Swedish. All this is going through Kenny's head as the man continues to stand, smiling down at him, taking an occasional puff on his cigar.

'I worked in a garage once,' he mumbles. 'And I helped with odd jobs as well as the gardening.' Why is he talking like this to a stranger? He has no idea what is going to happen next but doesn't feel afraid. Which surprises him.

Stefan

One morning, when Kenny had been at Stefan's flat for nearly a fortnight, he woke to find that he had slept through the night for the first time in months. From his skin he caught the faint odour, not of stale sweat and urine, but of soap and shampoo, thanks to the shower in Stefan's guest bathroom. (He had used the gold-tapped shower at Marit's on occasions, but she had preferred him to use her claw-foot bath, where she could watch him soap himself. This seemed to excite her and, watching her face in the mirror on the wall soften, he would quickly feel his own arousal. Which is what she often seemed to want.) There wasn't a shower back at his grandmother's little house. Just a small bath and sink and separate toilet. The first shower he'd come across was at secondary school when all the class had to strip off after football or athletics. He'd hated it. Everyone had to run through, pretending not to glance at each other's developing bodies. But using Stefan's shower was wonderful, once he had worked out which way to turn the controls. The walls were tiled in white except round the edges – they glowed with painted flowers and fruit. But most importantly for Kenny, it was private. Now he could be clean, without looking over his shoulder all the time. He no longer stank. And nor was he hungry. Stefan cooked food every day, and clearly loved doing it.

The plan, proposed by Stefan that freezing night under the railway arches, had been for Kenny to help Stefan with various household tasks in exchange for a place to stay and a small wage. He would do some basic flat-cleaning, take care of the plants on the small balcony, and start painting some window frames and skirting boards in the study, a job Stefan said he had been putting off for far too long.

Doing housework was fine. Kenny had always had to help Granny Sarah from when he was quite tiny. The painting was more problematic, but he quickly learned how to deal with the accidental drips of paint onto glass or floor with a rag and some turpentine. Getting a smooth surface, with no runs, took longer. Stefan encouraged him and seemed pleased. Kenny was also helping with food shopping now. Stefan went with him the first time to the market stall in Soho, piled high with huge Spanish onions, gleaming irregular-shaped tomatoes, and some things Kenny had never seen in Granny Sarah's Co-op or her corner shop. Stefan named them for him: purple aubergines, white garlic bulbs and orange capsicums. Marit had never taken him shopping, and her staff dealt with the cooking, so although he'd eaten well, he'd not seen such things in the raw. It had quickly become clear to Kenny that his work for Marit was either in the garden or in the bedroom, not in the kitchen.

Back at the flat after their first market jaunt, Stefan asked him to sit on a kitchen stool to watch carefully while he chopped things up with a very sharp knife on a wooden board. He poured olive oil into a large curved pan over a gas ring, then threw the chopped vegetables in, one at a time.

'You see, dear boy, you need to watch and learn. When you have been here a bit longer, I want you to be able to get proper employment. This is the key to your future. As a painter, or a chef maybe. And of course, you already understand about gardening, so you will have some choices. The world, as they say, will then be your oyster.' He looked up from the counter top where he was snipping leaves from a small green plant and smiled. Kenny smiled back. The idea of earning some proper money was a new thought. He watched the green leaves fall into the pan. Soon a delicious smell reached him. 'It's basil,' Stefan said, seeing his smile. 'It makes all the difference. Here, please keep this moving while I get the plates ready.'

Kenny took the wooden spoon from Stefan and stirred the mixture.

'When I first came here,' said Stefan, looking away from Kenny and up to the moulded ceiling, as if eye contact was uncomfortable, 'I knew very little and I had nothing.' Stefan wasn't smiling now. 'You know, Kenny, my dear, I too slept in an alley just like you, under an arch, or in a street doorway.'

'Gosh, Stefan, why? I can't imagine you on the pavement.'

'No? Well, it happened.' His attention came back to the pan of vegetables. 'But enough of that old history. Come, Kenny, we will eat now. Bring those fresh bread rolls and the salad bowl through to the dining room before this little concoction gets cold. Tomorrow's lesson will be how to make a stunning vinaigrette!'

They sat and ate in silence, but then, wiping the last bit of the vegetable stew from his plate with a piece of bread, Kenny asked, 'Stefan, what happened to you? How did you get off the street?' There was a pause, as Stefan took some time to wipe his own plate.

'Someone offered to help me. Someone kind,' Stefan said, as he collected the finished plates. Kenny just caught the quiet words, 'Someone kind who made a difference', as Stefan took the empty things to the kitchen. He didn't seem to want to say more.

One night in late November, Stefan took Kenny to a place called Jimmy's in Soho. It was a Greek restaurant down in a cellar. The sound of loud conversations, clinking glasses and scraping chairs grew, along with the smell of spicy food, as they walked down the stairs. Once seated at a small table, Kenny looked about at all the people talking loudly, gesticulating with forks, waving glasses or fingers in the air.

'The talk is usually about art, music or politics,' Stefan told him. 'Don't worry. These people like to argue while they eat and drink, even when they agree about almost everything. I know this, because I worked here as a waiter many years ago. More of that story another time. You mustn't have my whole history all in one go!' He pointed out a few faces, people, he said, who were quite well known. Members of Parliament, journalists, writers, actors. No one Kenny had heard of.

'Jimmy, the owner, is from Cyprus. And over there, look, the tall, fat guy shouting. It's the chef. He doesn't know the meaning of quiet!'

Over a meal of spicy meat covered with a layer of cheese, (moussaka, Stefan said), fat chips, salad with pieces of white cheese lurking among the leaves, and then sweet, honeyed little squares washed down with harsh red wine that made Kenny's head swim, Stefan told him about coming to London from Poland in 1946. He'd come with nothing, he said, had got away after a long and difficult journey as the Iron Curtain fell.

'I've never gone back but, Kenny, do you know? – I dream often of my old home. I can wake in tears, even now after so long.'

Kenny had never heard a man talk like this. Not that he's known many men, not to have a proper conversation with. The garage owner who'd employed him for that short time in Southsea only talked football and girls, Bert the gardener said almost nothing, although his face often spoke volumes, a few teachers at his school just used to shout, or ignore him, and the various grumpy antique dealers he had met in Yorkshire spoke without ever looking him in the eye.

Here, among the hubbub of argumentative conviviality, Stefan looked at home, smiling at the world around him, speaking expansively. He seemed to be saying whatever came into his head, switching rapidly from a description of his early life in Poland to current politics, which was something else Kenny didn't know about, but he was enjoying watching Stefan's mobile, energised face. He had already decided that Stefan was someone who was kind, who seemed to want nothing from him but his company and some help in the flat. He hadn't asked him too many questions and Kenny felt safe.

'So, what do you think, Kenny?' He realised Stefan was asking him something. 'What will America do now, with Lyndon Johnson in charge? I'm still so shocked, aren't you? Just when the world seemed to be getting a bit safer.'

It was clear from Kenny's face that he hadn't followed all these events.

'I don't know, Stefan. I got so out of the habit of following the news,' he said, looking up at Stefan's puzzled face. 'I saw things on the newspaper placards in the West End. Sometimes I'd pick up an old paper someone had dropped on the pavement, or stuffed in a bin.' Reading the papers had made him wonder: millions of papers printed each day, the same words read by him and how many thousands of others? Even perhaps by Gemma, wherever she was now. She could have read some of the very same stories he had. He liked that thought.

Stefan was still talking about the last extraordinary year. He was trying to explain about the terrifying days last autumn when American and Russian warships were sailing towards each other in the Atlantic, about the signs of a political thaw in the summer allowing a general willingness to call a halt to weapons testing. Something important had been signed in Moscow in the summer, which had been a sign of new hope for the world until the dreadful gunning down of the young president.

'Didn't you hear any news up in Yorkshire, Kenny?'

'Not a lot. There was an old radio in the house, but Marit always switched it off if I came into the room so I only caught snatches, odd names that got repeated,' Kenny said quietly, looking down, playing a little with his cutlery. 'I think there must have been one in Marit's office as well, but I wasn't allowed in there.' He sipped a bit more wine, thinking how pathetic these words sounded now. How to begin to talk about the time with Marit? How to explain the embarrassment and shame he now felt at how he had allowed her to cut him off from everything? How she had even forbidden him to talk to any of the visitors when, for a few days a month, the gardens were open to the public.

*

The next Saturday, Kenny and Stefan were sitting at a small round table in an Italian restaurant in Soho, after shopping for vegetables in the street market and buying a specially rolled cut of pork from the French butcher in Old Compton Street. Stefan had explained to Kenny that he was looking forward to stuffing the joint with prunes, before tying it up and roasting it with some potatoes. They would then eat it with a simple green salad and vinaigrette, which Kenny would be making under his instructions.

'It will be delicious,' he said with a smile. 'And you must watch carefully while I do this, so you can remember for the future. You are a quick learner, but if we are to make a proper cook of you, you must also pay attention and not slide off into one of your daydreams.'

Stefan had ordered for them both, after a small exchange of pleasantries with the waiter who obviously knew him as a regular. A small avocado salad with vinaigrette, followed by something called saltimbocca, which meant 'jump into the mouth', Stefan explained. They were already eating some stuffed olives and drinking from a small carafe of red wine, which caught the back of Kenny's throat as he took his first sip, before it started to warm him from the inside. When the main course arrived, Stefan was talking enthusiastically, between mouthfuls, about cooking.

'Italian is not like Polish, of course. The seasoning is so different, but it is delicious in a different way. Now, tell me, dear boy, can you identify the various flavours in this dish?'

Kenny had become used to Stefan's tests in the few weeks since he had been living in the flat. 'Kenny', he'd said, after the first few days, 'you are going to be my apprentice in the kitchen. You must learn about flavours and textures and timings. All are important.' Kenny had quickly learned to recognise basil and appreciate what its presence could do to tomato dishes, and knew that you had to watch for just the right moment to be sure the chopped onion and garlic cooking in the olive oil would be ready for the addition of the tablespoons of Arborio rice for a risotto. But there was something challenging him now as he cut into the saltimbocca. Stefan was watching him intently as Kenny tried to identify the taste.

'Some kind of herb, not basil. Is it thyme?'

'No. It is sage. If you look you can see how the veal is wrapped in something before cooking. The sage is inside with a slice of prosciutto. And of course, the sauce has wine in it. The Italians have a way of magically putting different flavours together…like your bacon and eggs.' He smiled at his own joke and Kenny smiled with him. 'Are you enjoying, Kenny?'

'Yes, it's amazing. Not like anything I've eaten before. But I do remember seeing sage growing in the garden up in Yorkshire. I was supposed to learn the names of everything from Bert, the old gardener there.'

Kenny remembered, but didn't say, that Marit could suddenly quiz him to test him about his plant knowledge. But he hadn't felt like an apprentice. More like a slave, he often thought, now he was free of her.

Stefan's voice broke into his reflections. 'Now, Kenny, I want you to tell me about the book you were looking at this morning before we came out. It is quite old, I think. And quite famous too?'

Kenny had been holding, flicking through pages without reading, the copy of Hans Christian Andersen stories that he'd been carrying with him since he left his house in Crane Street – hidden under his bed at Coldwater Hall, at the bottom of his rucksack when he was hitch-hiking down to London, under his head while the rucksack was his only pillow on the pavement and under the arches.

'Oh, it's nothing, just something I've had for ages. An old friend gave it to me one birthday when I was very young. Well, it's just a children's book really.'

'Just a children's book, Kenny?' Stefan was sitting up in his chair, both palms on the white, crisp tablecloth in front of him. He was getting that enlivened look about him that Kenny recognised. 'Dear boy, there is a wealth of truth in these old children's stories. You do know that some of these tales have travelled round the world for centuries, passed along by travelling person to travelling person. And why? Children's literature comes from adult minds and has lasted because it shines a light sideways on some universal dilemmas and experiences, and it does so as a way of helping children to recognise some things in their own lives that they don't yet have words for. Children's books are an education for all ages, and always have been.' Looking as if he'd run out of steam, Stefan sat back in his chair, and his usual smile returned. 'And who gave you this lovely book?'

For a second Kenny couldn't speak. Something seemed to be catching in his throat, and he coughed, before continuing. 'A girl called Gemma. She lived over the road from me and we played…did a lot of things together when we were small.' He didn't know if he wanted to say more and was relieved when the waiter appeared to take away their plates and to ask if they would like a dessert.

'What shall we have, Kenny? I think maybe not too much as we will eat tonight. How about some exquisite Italian ice cream and a small espresso?' The waiter nodded to show he had heard and disappeared again on silent feet. 'So, tell me about this Gemma. She must have liked you very much to give you this book. Where is Gemma now?'

Kenny searched for his last image of her. Was it when he'd seen her walking past the garage in her brown school uniform, beret on the side of her head? She hadn't seen him lying half under that old Ford Consul. Or was it when he'd bumped into her, arm in arm with her friend Julie? If so, he'd probably said, or maybe just thought, something unkind.

'Stefan, I couldn't say. She was always much better at school than me and so I expect she went off to college somewhere. Or moved away. I told you, it's ages since I went home.'

'Yes, I remember.' Kenny felt Stefan's eyes on him. Looking up he saw that he wasn't smiling. 'Yes, Kenny. And I have wondered why. You are a private young man, on the whole, and I will not push you. I am also private about many things and will not be pushed. But I will say this.' Stefan paused, looking down to brush a few crumbs off the table. 'Don't leave things too long or you may regret...' Stefan was frowning and looking away now, towards the light from the window, suddenly interested in the streams of traffic and people moving up and down the street. 'Yes. Leave it too long and you can find you have dropped the threads of something important. And then all you can do is feel sad.' His voice dropped. It was as if Stefan was talking to himself as the waiter reappeared with the small glass dishes containing three scoops of pink, green and brown ice cream, each dish topped with a crisp wafer.

'Italian ice cream is the best. Even better than Polish,' Stefan said brightly, as he took a spoonful to his mouth and the conversation seemed over.

*

137

Next morning, when Kenny emerged for breakfast, he was surprised to find a carefully wrapped parcel by his plate.

'What's this, Stefan?' he asked as he started to unwrap it. Inside, he found three books. *Brighton Rock* by Graham Greene, *Brideshead Revisited* by Evelyn Waugh and *Animal Farm* by George Orwell. He looked up, questioningly, at Stefan who appeared to be concentrating hard on his scrambled eggs on toast.

'Time to read some grown-up books as well as children's, Kenny. Let me know when you have finished one, and we will have a grown-up discussion. Even the best chefs and gardeners need to be well informed.'

A few nights later, when Kenny was drinking a mug of tea in the kitchen, having just finished the painting job in the study, Stefan came through the front door, full of breathless excitement and called out, 'Kenny, you need to get yourself well cleaned up and dressed properly. I'm taking you out for a real treat. A reward for all your hard work. We are going to hear some fantastic music.'

While Kenny was looking at his only two shirts, wondering which of them was the least-worst, Stefan tapped on his bedroom door and came in holding out a velvet jacket and a flowery tie.

'It's a bit of a smart place this club. I don't want the man on the door turning you away.' Stefan smiled at his own joke, eyes crinkling at each side. 'So, if you don't mind, just try this on. It's an old one of mine and too small for me. I like cake too much for my waist.'

They took a taxi to a side street in Soho. Above the entrance to the club hung a glowing sign of a saxophone. Stefan pulled some notes from his leather wallet to pay, and they went down a short flight of steps, emerging into a large room already crowded with people sitting in the almost dark, their faces only slightly lit by table lamps. A few spotlights focused on the stage where a group of black musicians sat or stood. A young man wearing an over-large cap was picking at a double bass, a much older man sat fingering the keys of a piano and a very large ungainly man in a brightly coloured and patterned shirt, eyes hidden by dark glasses, was breathing into a flute. Various other instruments hung round his neck at the same time as if waiting to be needed. Kenny wasn't clear if the musicians were tuning up or had really started to play. It was not like any kind of music he'd heard before, but then the old pianist reached for the microphone and announced, in a gravelly voice, the name of a tune. There was clapping from around the room and then they were off at a great pace. Kenny began to feel as if the instruments were talking to each other and to him. The musical conversation rose to a crescendo and someone in the audience shouted out "yeah" and clapped, then others joined in, even though it was clearly not the end of the tune. He glanced at Stefan who was looking so happy, watching the stage intently, just occasionally looking back towards Kenny to see if he was enjoying it too.

In the interval Kenny went off to find the gents. On his way back to his seat, he saw that a couple of well-dressed men were talking to Stefan. The musicians were coming back onto the small stage, and Stefan and the men quickly ended their conversation and embraced. Kenny felt uncomfortable. As they started to return to their seats, something about him seemed to raise question marks in their faces as they turned back to wave goodbye to Stefan.

Back at the flat, Kenny was walking ahead of Stefan as they entered the hallway. When he felt a hand on the back of his neck, he froze, but it was immediately removed and Stefan went quickly to his own room, calling goodnight over his shoulder, before shutting his door firmly.

On Christmas morning, Kenny was already eating his cornflakes when Stefan tiptoed in, a bit theatrically, and placed a tissue-paper-wrapped parcel by his plate, with rather a schoolboy's eager expression.

'Happy Christmas, dear boy, and let us hope the coming year will bring you better fortune. And maybe this will help.' Unwrapping the parcel, Kenny found a plain, light-blue jumper in the softest wool.

'Gosh, Stefan. This is really nice and I'm sorry, I haven't got you anything.' Stefan waved his apology away.

'Wash it carefully. It's cashmere. Not too hot or you will ruin it, and that would be a terrible waste. When you've had breakfast, you should try it on in case the size isn't right.'

In his room, Kenny slipped the jumper over his head and looked at himself in front of the dressing-table mirror. Seeing Stefan's reflected face appear, smiling from behind him suddenly brought back Marit's smiling image in the bathroom mirror on his first night at Coldwater Hall. Kenny's smile shrank and Stefan quickly turned away, heading back to the kitchen where Kenny heard him noisily washing the breakfast plates.

'I'm making more coffee when you are ready, Kenny,' he called from the kitchen.

Who's There?

Darkness fell earlier and earlier as Gemma's term was drawing to a close. As she stepped off the corporation bus, a weariness gathered around her shoulders like one of Birmingham's heavy fogs. It slid whispering into her head to mingle with her longing for home. She was laden with food shopping, library books and a folder of messy course notes, which she planned on turning into an essay once she got back to Southsea. Already picturing her mother's presence in the warm, safe kitchen, she found herself at the door of the shared student house, and her key was turning in the lock. After shouldering the front door open, ready to drop her bags in the little hall and shed her heavy winter coat, she stood, stopped in her tracks by the familiar but unexpected smell of Bruce's aftershave. She was sure she hadn't spotted his car. He must have parked round the corner. Hearing the noise of saucepans and humming coming from the kitchen, she hung her coat on the banister and set the book bags by the sitting room door. With the shopping bag in one hand, she put on a pleased smile and, consciously slowing her breath, turned the handle of the kitchen door.

Gemma was still smiling at Bruce as he turned round from the stove. She also rapidly checked his facial expression and the way he was holding his body, in the way now habitual with her. She threw a quick glance round the kitchen, noticing the half-empty bottle of red wine and the glass next to it. She knew she'd need to be careful.

'Gemma, darling, you're back already. Oh Lord, I thought I'd have got all this done by the time you arrived. Welcome to my little surprise supper party.'

'Hi Bruce, it's lovely to see you, but I thought…you'd said you were coming up tomorrow evening. How did you get in?' For a millisecond she saw the shadow of disappointment on his face.

'The lovely Imogen, of course. She was just leaving when I turned up and she kindly let me in. She said Ruth had already gone off home. They'd both finished lectures for the term and so were making an early getaway. Is that a problem?' Bruce moved towards her, fetching a glass from the shelf and filling it from the bottle on the table, before handing it to her. 'You might look a bit pleased to see me when I've travelled all day to be here and cook my poor darling student girlfriend her supper.'

'Oh Bruce, of course I'm pleased but just not expecting… I mean, yes, a lovely surprise. Did you come on the train? I didn't see your car.'

'No train. Drove here, so impatient to see my dear girl! The street was full, so I'm parked in the next street.'

'Ah, I see. Well, something smells delicious.' Be careful, she suddenly thought, not knowing why. 'What are we having for supper then?'

'One of my speciality pasta sauces. Lots of onion, garlic, tomato, mince and a tiny *bouquet garni*. I was getting the sauce ready first as I wasn't sure what time you'd be back. And I've made a salad, so all that's left is to boil water for the spaghetti and we'll be ready to sit down and enjoy it. And each other's company, sweetheart. How I have missed you.'

'You are such a wizard in the kitchen, Bruce, but in honour of your cooking prowess, I must have a wash and change into something worthy of your surprise. Won't be long.'

'OK sweetheart, and you know I'd love to come and help you with all of that, but I mustn't let the sauce spoil.'

Upstairs, Gemma peeled off her long boots, before exchanging her skirt and cardigan for a new pair of Levi's and her black polo-neck jumper. In the tiny bathroom she stood by the sink to quickly wash away the Birmingham grime with her soapy flannel. Looking into the glass she wondered who she was seeing. She tried to smooth out the frown, attempted a smile, but it didn't convince. She knew she was tired – knew she'd been looking forward to a night on her own – wanted to have space and time to think about seeing her mother again. She was longing to be back in Southsea, to be able to stride along the seafront in a December blast of salty air, hearing the grinding of the pebbles being pushed around by the thrust and drag of the waves, and to feel looked after unconditionally by her mother.

'Gemma, it's all ready,' Bruce called up the stairs. 'How long are you going to be up there titivating?' Turning away from the mirror, with a sigh, barefooted she crossed the cold lino, thinking, I'm not walking on lino – I'm walking on eggshells, and headed downstairs to the kitchen.

*

Gemma's face was aching with her effort to keep Bruce happy. He'd finished off the first bottle and was well into the next one. He never visited her without bringing gifts. Flowers, perfume and wine. Lots of wine. It seemed extravagant to her, but now that he had finished his engineering course in Portsmouth and was no longer on a grant – he was working in London in some office, and earning – he said he could afford to spoil her. She knew by now about his well-off family. She'd listened sympathetically, for hours, to his tales about the boarding schools, about the absentee parents in Hong Kong, and the miserable holiday visits with school friends and their reluctant relatives. She'd guessed at the sadness and the envy written between his lines about success in cricket and rugby, the wonders of the skiing trips with the school, his pride in his army cadet uniform. With this background information, she'd tried really hard to sympathetically make sense of his contradictions, often thinking later that she'd been maybe too understanding, making too many excuses for his moodiness and sudden outbursts of jealousy.

'Why don't you tell me about your day, sweetheart? Good one?'

She realised she was being asked a question. Careful what you say. He's had a lot of wine. So easy to say the wrong thing and upset him.

'Tiring, really. End-of-term stuff. Taking books back to the library, searching round for new ones. Checking out next term's tutorial dates. You know the kind of thing.' She got up and, picking up the scraped, sticky pasta plates, cutlery and glasses, moved towards the sink, but before she'd got the things into the plastic bowl, Bruce's voice cut in.

'Hey, where's my wine glass?'

'Sorry, Bruce, I thought you'd finished. Just wanted to clear things, as you'd done all the lovely cooking, so we can go and put our feet up on the sofa.' Will that work?

'Did I say I'd finished?' He was frowning at her as she turned round from the sink.

'Here you are. Sorry about that.' Gemma poured another glass from the half-empty bottle on the sideboard. Passing it back to Bruce, she tried distracting him.

'What do you feel like doing tomorrow? There's a good film on at the Odeon in town. That new one people have been talking about. *It's a Mad, Mad, Mad World.* We could go to the matinee and then go on for a nice meal in New Street.'

'Are you sure you can spare the time for me? Won't you be needing to pack ready for going to see dear Mummy?'

'Oh, Bruce, you know I have to go. I promised her ages ago. We've talked about this.'

Gemma, leaning against the counter top, knew he was cross about her trip home for Christmas without him. He'd wanted her to go with him to meet his family, who were now retired and living somewhere in Sussex. They'd been through this so many times on the phone. She'd explained how Elizabeth had sounded tired, in low spirits recently. Gemma hadn't been home since Sarah's funeral and, without being demanding, Elizabeth had made it clear how much she'd like her daughter to share Christmas with her. Turning back to the sink, Gemma started washing dishes, energetically rubbing the remains of the pasta from the plates with the squeegee mop. For a moment it was quiet, apart from the slop of the soapy water in front of her, and the chink of the plates as she stacked them on the metal drainer. For a moment she was aware of the kitchen clock, ticking the seconds away on the wall. For a moment she wondered if Bruce had silently stood and gone away.

'So, Gemma, who are you going to miss over Christmas?'

'You, of course, Bruce', she said, trying to sound convincing. She just wanted to get through this evening without an all-out row. The egg shells were pressing harder into her feet.

'Not that man I saw you talking to this afternoon? The chap in the trench coat and red scarf?'

'How…what… Bruce, what are you talking about?'

But Gemma knew exactly who he was talking about. Gerry Barker. Her lovely, kind tutor. He'd called out to her from the path, just as she was coming down the library steps, arms clutching the heavy wodge of books all ready to take home to help with her assignments. Hearing his call, she'd changed course towards where he stood waiting, with his usual big smile, his old battered briefcase in one nicotine-stained hand, his familiar red scarf wound haphazardly round his neck. He always seemed pleased to see her, and she could still be taken by surprise by his warmth. Maybe it was because he seemed to see more in her than she could see in herself.

'That sounds like my tutor, Gerry Barker. But how did you…? I thought you'd driven straight here.' She could feel her heart rate speeding up. She hid her shaking hands behind her back as she leaned against the sink. 'I bumped into him outside the library after changing my books, and he stopped me to check something about my next essay. But why on earth…?'

'Well, I decided to get up here early and surprise you, as you are supposed to be my girlfriend, who has eyes only for me, but it seems I was wrong.' Bruce suddenly stood up. The noise of his chair scraping back set her teeth on edge like nails on a blackboard. 'You seemed to be having such a jolly chat with Mr Red Scarf, so not wanting to break up your little party, I changed my mind and came on here.'

'Do you mean you were spying on me, Bruce? Is that what you're telling me?'

'Not spying, what a thing to say, just checking to see if I can trust you.' He was smiling at her. How can a person look so cruel while smiling? 'Looks like I was right. I could see how you and he were looking at each other. Maybe he's going to be turning up in Southsea as a great big Christmas present for you on Christmas morning!'

Gemma turned back to the sink, trying to stop the shaking. Picking up the mop, she started to rewash an already-clean plate, trying to lose herself in the tiny gleam of the soap bubbles. She heard his footsteps seconds before feeling the pain as he yanked her hair from behind, pulling her shoulder at the same time to spin her round, and then she was against the kitchen wall, aware of the clock ticking loudly near her right ear, and she could smell the red wine and garlic on his breath as he pushed his face up against hers.

The clock was still ticking on the kitchen wall. It was well past midnight. Bruce was stretched out on the sofa in the living room asleep, passed out, thank goodness. Gemma was staring at her reflection in the glass pane of the back door. How long had she been standing here? Five minutes? An hour?

She could already see the marks appearing on her neck. The tracks of tears through her make-up had dried.

Tiptoeing shoeless upstairs, she went into the bedroom, took her suitcase from on top of the wardrobe, and her old rucksack from the hook on the door, and started to pack.

On the Run

As Gemma settled into her seat on the train, the smell of the thick Birmingham fog was still with her, clinging to her coat. It seemed to have taken up permanent residence in her nostrils, and its acrid taste lingered in her mouth.

She'd walked most of the way into town in the dark, dragging her hastily filled case in one hand, and with her old rucksack full of books and folders on her back. She'd been so full of energy, whether from her rage or fear, or both, that it hadn't seemed to take long. It had in fact taken over an hour as she'd thrown one foot in front of the other, hearing her own footfall in front of her while straining to hear if any larger, heavier feet were coming from behind.

Not noticing the dark, bare branches of the trees along the edge of the park, but looking ahead as each junction got nearer, scanning the next corner for any sign of a shadowy figure waiting to grab her. She was not just furious at Bruce's behaviour now. She was seriously frightened of him.

Gemma had felt uneasy about Bruce often enough in the past few weeks, but now he had lost control so viciously, her understanding was crystallising, the danger he posed now in focus. How had she allowed him to persuade her again and again that he really cared for her, that his jealousy was only stemming from love? How had he convinced her that, somehow, without him she would be nothing. Made her think it was a flaw in her, something permanently missing.

Reaching the centre of the city, a few early pedestrians and cars made her feel less alone, and she became aware of her breathing, trying to slow it down. The sudden sound of shutters rolling up on a newsagent's frontage made her jump, but then reassured her, as she saw the shop lights shining on shelves of cigarettes, displays of chocolate bars and peanuts, the stacked piles of the day's newspapers ready to be released and dispersed. Ordinary things. Turning up the hill to the station, she caught sight of a handful of starlings as they flashed across a slight streak of grey in the sky. The night was over at last.

During the long, cold wait on the platform, her energy and anger had quickly drained away, keeping pace with her dropping body temperature. The shuttered café offered nothing, although someone was clattering with cups and saucers and plates ready for opening. For a moment, hearing the platform clock strike seven, she wondered what she was doing there. Then putting a hand under her big woollen scarf to her neck, remembering, she found herself looking along the platform, twice each way, like a child doing the green cross code. But not looking out for cars. Looking out for Bruce. A porter strolling along, looking at his watch and fingering his flag, was a reassurance. A sudden flash, an image of Bruce spreadeagled on the sofa next to his empty bottle, filled her vision. But what if Bruce had woken and found she'd gone? What would he do? He'd be angry, for sure. Angry enough to get in his car? He was so drunk last night he'd find that difficult, and she had a sudden wish that he'd crash, or be stopped by the police. Was she going mad?

At seven twenty the train rumbled into the station and Gemma got up, stiff with having sat so long in the cold. After a grateful look at the porter, who lifted her case onto the carriage, she found a seat and collapsed into it. Sitting on the train now, her mind was a blank as she circled her ankles and rubbed her arms to get her circulation going. Then for a few moments she tried to peer out through the dingy window beside her into the half-lit city, but her eyes drooped and she was soon asleep.

When a hand touched her on her shoulder, she woke suddenly with a gasp, ready to scream, ready to run.

'It's all right, love!' said a deep brummy voice. 'Got your ticket handy?'

The tall figure bending over her was older than Bruce. Was brown-skinned and moustached. Wearing a uniform. Wasn't Bruce. Wasn't him. She began to breathe properly again.

'Sorry, my love. Didn't mean to give you a shock. You look like you've seen a ghost.'

'No, it's OK. Just was fast asleep. Late night, you know.'

'Certainly do. Nearly Christmastime. People still stumblin' round 'alf-cut near the town hall when I was comin' to work this morning. But you sure you're OK? Maybe you should get yourself a hot drink. It's not far. Just pop along there and you'll find it in the next-but-one coach.'

'Thanks. I think I will.'

*

Standing, staring out of the window into a lighter world now rushing past, Gemma clutched her hot tea with both hands. Why did she feel like crying with surprise when older men spoke kindly to her as if she was a nice person? That old gardener in Yorkshire. He'd noticed how she was feeling – how cold she was. Like that ticket collector. Like her tutor when they'd been talking outside the library. He'd been so encouraging and interested in her essay ideas. She shivered as she thought of how Bruce had been standing there watching them all the time. And again Bruce, inside her head, clinging to her thinking like the Birmingham fog. When she'd tried to end it with him after the row in the Yorkshire pub, she'd felt so sure. Quite sure that he had got her wrong. Quite sure that he'd hurt her. And yet she'd let him back. How the hell did that happen? As if she couldn't believe she could stand on her own two feet. And might it happen again? She tried to remember that weekend when he'd shown up at her door with flowers. How had he found out her new address? She'd really tried to get away from him, hadn't she? That weak spot in her make-up he always sensed, that fear of being on her own, of being unseen, that experience of disappearing into herself to the point of extinction. He had always recognised that. He recognised it. It wasn't that he thought she was lovely, sexy, clever. It was that he could control her.

A Piece of Glass

Waking on the sofa, his face stuffed into a cushion, and smelling his own stale breath, Bruce called croakily for Gemma, as he raised his head slightly listening to the silence in the house. Maybe she'd gone for fresh bread and milk from the corner shop. Raising himself further on one elbow, and looking about the room, his head and stomach swam with an urgency that propelled him to the small cloakroom in the hall where he vomited loudly and fully. Red wine, spaghetti bolognese and more red wine spewed out, splashing into the toilet bowl. The smell of it made him even more nauseated, and he retreated into the kitchen, listening out for Gemma's key in the door, hoping for the warm smell of fresh bread and soon, coffee.

The sight of the kitchen's devastation brought him to a halt. A chair turned over, shards of glass, chips of china, scattered cutlery on the linoleum. Something awful had gone on here. And where was Gemma? Not even a sign of a note. As he searched around for a clean plate and cup, he tried to piece together the fragments from the previous evening. He had spent ages cooking, he remembered. She should have been more appreciative! He'd gone to all that trouble.

Dragging himself up the narrow stairs, half on his knees and pulling on the banisters, he reached her room. Her bed neat was clearly unslept in. Her bedside book gone. Glancing up to the top of the wardrobe, the absence of her old suitcase stared back at him. In the bathroom. No toothbrush, no make-up bag. Unable to take it in, he struggled back downstairs. Why hadn't he noticed before that her rucksack and book bag were no longer sitting on the floor by the bottom stair?

Bruce filled the kettle with water and set it on the gas ring, impatient for coffee, and put two slices of bread under the grill before sitting down, head in hands. Hazy recollections swam in and out of focus until one bright piece of truth came to the fore.

He'd hurt her. He'd hurt his Gemma. There was a brief glimmer of guilt, of sadness before his rage rose up like his vomit had done, but this he couldn't throw away as easily.

She'd made him do it. Why hadn't she been more loving? She'd been cold. Yes, that was it. Cold and nasty, accusing him of spying on her when he'd only gone to try and meet her as a nice surprise. And there she'd been, smiling sweetly, chatting with that man in the red scarf outside the library. She hadn't even noticed him standing there by that tree. He'd felt invisible while his girlfriend had been clearly flirting with another man. So, of course he'd been justifiably angry, especially when he tackled her. He'd been careful to cook first and even waited until they'd eaten and she'd dared to pretend that it wasn't important because it was one of her teachers!

Bruce poured hot water onto the spoonful of coffee in a mug, cursed as the smell of burning toast reached him, and trod back, in his still bare feet, onto a splinter of glass. As he yelled out, a spike of a memory shot through him. At boarding school. He would have been about seven years old. Stepping out of his narrow bed in the night to go for a pee, he'd trodden on something sharp. A piece of china maybe? He couldn't remember exactly but could feel again, along with the biting pain, a wish for someone to come, to feel his mother's arms around him, comforting as they'd been before they had sent him away to school. She had put her arms around him when she was helping him onto the train. Him all smart with his new school uniform carrying his little suitcase, but for the first time it hadn't felt a comfort. She'd been crying a bit but he'd made sure he held his own tears back. All he'd felt was confusion, coloured with fear and rage.

Hobbling over to the sink, Bruce tried to raise his foot up to the tap to wash away the blood, and the image came from nowhere of Jackie Kennedy, cradling her dying husband, while blood soaked into her neat little pink suit. Only a few weeks ago. A president shot in full view of the world's cameras. Out of the blue. He and Gemma had talked on the phone that night. Where the bloody hell was she now?

God, now his mind was wandering. He tried to focus on his foot. The bleeding was easing off now. Standing on one leg, he hopped to the cupboard where he knew there were plasters. He'd seen Gemma get some out last time he'd visited, after she'd cut her finger. He'd put the plaster on gently after washing her finger carefully under the tap. Now he felt both empty and angry at having to get his own plaster and put it on his foot himself. The feelings nearly swamped him.

Where was Gemma? He shouldn't have to be doing this himself. Someone, Mother, Matron or Gemma should be on hand to help him. It was what he deserved. Surely!

An hour later, dressed but neither washed nor shaved, Bruce let himself out of the front door, leaving behind the littered scene of violence in the kitchen and the silence of the empty house.

Part Five

Boxing Day

It's Boxing Day. Or it will be when it gets light. Bruce wakes in his old bed in his parents' home in Sussex. He feels like he hasn't slept but still feels the drift of nightmares that haven't quite gone away. He'd been cross and miserable all through Christmas Day. Gemma should have been here. With me!

His parents had been expecting her to arrive. He'd felt so sure he'd be able to persuade her. But no. She'd been stubborn. Mean even! Why? Because of her mum or someone else? The man in the red scarf? An old boyfriend in Southsea? That chap, she'd said, was just a friend – the one who'd sent a card.

He is beset with contradictory imagined scenarios. Of him at her door in Southsea, with flowers and presents and protestations of love, to be greeted with fulsome apologies and grateful affection…and passion maybe? Or of arriving to find a strange car outside her door, of hearing music and singing from behind closed curtains, seeing shadows of a couple close together and finding evidence of her utter betrayal of their relationship.

He knows he's annoyed his parents by drinking too much wine at dinner, snapping at them when they started asking about Gemma.

'Tell us about her then, darling.'

'Yes, when can we meet her? It's so disappointing that she couldn't come after all.'

'She looks absolutely lovely in her photographs.'

He'd gone on steadily drinking after they'd scuttled off to bed. Had sat slumped on the sofa, eyes wandering over the cards strung above the mantlepiece on a red satin ribbon. Then to the framed images on each side of the fireplace. Pictures of places they had been to and he hadn't. All those places they had enjoyed while he'd spent school holidays feeling he was unwanted and in the way in the homes of school friends. His parents had posted him presents, but often the clothes were the wrong size, emphasising that they really didn't know who he was or what he needed. And over on the other side of the sofa, on the piano, the framed photo of him with Gemma, taken by a friend in Southsea right by the harbour entrance outside the Still and West. The old pub he had taken Gemma to on their first date.

He is awake now and, although unsteady on his feet, through a brandy haze he manages to wash, shave without cutting himself, and find some clean clothes.

He is going to take Gemma her Christmas present. It will be a day late but never mind. He will apologise. She'll be so delighted to see him.

Dressed and downstairs, making coffee, he is wishing his head would stop swimming. He will need to drive with the windows open in spite of the cold. He looks out of the window and sees the thick frost covering the roof of his car. It won't take long for him to cut across to pick up the A3 and then in no time he will be racing through the gap in the South Downs and on to the coast. And to Gemma. He pictures them sitting with mugs of coffee, and maybe some toast, in her mother's little kitchen. She'll be sleepy and surprised but relieved to see him. Bruce can already hear the conversation as they each apologise and promise to put it all behind them. He'll ask her to come back with him to meet his parents...

There's no one about as he gets in the car. It has taken a bit of time to scrape the ice off the windows, and his fingers feel raw. He has left his driving gloves in the house, but no time to be going back for them. He needs to get going. The beautifully wrapped parcel, a dress for Gemma from that expensive little shop in Petersfield, is on the passenger seat next to him. He has thrown his holdall onto the seat behind him.

The car is reluctant to start. As he fumbles with the key and the pedals, he's remembering his first driving lesson. Squirming at his father's impatience. The feeling of stupidity as he tried and failed to coordinate all the actions. His father's theatrical sighs. Suddenly the engine roars into life. An upstairs window opens and, twisting his head and looking up, he sees his mother's anxious face.

'Bruce! Where on earth are you going? It's the middle of the night.'

But he is already backing out of the drive and turning towards the main road and the signs to Portsmouth.

Half an hour later, Bruce is well on the way, driving at speed down the empty A3, windows wide open to keep awake, one hand on the wheel and one gently stroking the parcel on the seat beside him. He glances down, picturing the moment when Gemma will hold up the dress against herself with pleasure. When he feels the wheels begin to slip on the ice, he tries to right things, but in a panic oversteers. As the car spins out of his control onto the wrong side of the road, he sees the terrified driver's face in the cab of the lorry that is rushing towards him… and then nothing.

It's still dark. The last bits of debris are being removed from the London-bound carriageway of the A3. A red ACCIDENT AHEAD sign warns drivers to slow down although the lorry has already been taken away on a trailer, and its shocked driver lies in a bed in a Portsmouth hospital, concussed and bruised. Luckily, he was wearing his seat belt when the car came careering over the road in front of him.

A crumpled tangle of metal remains at the edge of the road. Nearby, blue lights flash rhythmically as two police officers wait by their patrol car for the pick-up truck to arrive and remove the wreckage. One of them is looking down at the parcel in his gloved hands. It is wrapped with holly-leaf paper and red ribbon and, apart from a smear of mud, appears unscathed.

'Windows must have been open, Fred,' the officer says, looking up at his partner, who stamps his feet in the cold. 'Would you fucking believe it? Must have got thrown out on impact.'

'Why the hell would anyone have windows open in this temperature, John?'

'Stank of booze, didn't he? Trying to keep awake maybe?'

'You think he might have dropped off? Not going to wake up now, is he? Mad geezer.'

'Probably belting home after a Christmas do. Bloody waste though. Apart from the fact that he's spoiled my morning.

Driving down the A3 in the middle of the night pissed like a bat out of hell.'

An older man, a witness, who had been obviously shaken to come upon the crash, has told them that the wrecked car had overtaken him a few miles back, going at least ninety.

The officer looks down again at the parcel. Shining his torch down he reads the little label, tied on with scrap of silver string: To my darling Gemma from Bruce with all my love. Happy Christmas.

'Poor Gemma, whoever she may be. She'll be waking up to a bad day, then.'

'Don't bear thinking about! God, I wish that bloody truck'd hurry. It's brass monkeys standing here,' says the other officer, who is holding the wallet from the dead driver's pocket. 'At least there's some identification on the poor bastard, which will help with the paperwork.'

'Right. There is that. Someone will still have to go round to tell the family at some point, but not me. I'm for a bacon sarnie and a big mug of strong coffee in the canteen as soon as I've got this stuff logged.'

It's Boxing Day morning and at breakfast Stefan suggests a walk to Hyde Park. As they stroll along the side of a lake, past people old and young sprawled in deckchairs in spite of the cold, Kenny thinks how much has changed since he used to sleep in one of those same chairs. Later, after eating ice-cream cornets, they stop for a moment on the edge of an ever-shifting crowd at Speakers' Corner. Kenny notices Stefan lifting his head suddenly. A loud voice is speaking a foreign language a few rows in front of them and Stefan is off, disappearing into the crowd and returning, clasping with both hands the arms of the owner of the loud voice, and speaking to him in the same language. Coming back to Kenny's side, he thrusts some notes into his hand, and tells him he should get a cab home, help himself to whatever is in the fridge, and do whatever else he likes. He's met his very old friend Pauli from Warsaw, and they are going to go and have an enormous meal at Daquise, the Polish restaurant by South Kensington station. This is bound to take many hours and require many glasses of red wine and probably some Bison Vodka.

Kenny decides to walk back, rather than get a cab. He strolls along Oxford Street looking in all the shop windows and then turning by Selfridges, heads north to the flat. A taxi would be a waste of money on such a nice day. Back in the flat, he feels the space around him and welcomes it. He hasn't had much time alone since meeting Stefan, who has mostly worked at home, either at the table in the dining room or, since the paint smell has mostly disappeared, in his study. To be here on his own feels like luxury to Kenny. Spreading himself out on the sofa, he starts to read *Brighton Rock*, but starts to nod a bit. Checking the clock, he thinks if he's quick, he'll have time to have a long soak in the big bath in Stefan's bathroom. He hasn't had a bath since leaving Coldwater Hall.

Dozing in the sweet-smelling, bubbly water he hears the front door opening and leaps out of the bath and is grabbing one of the huge, fluffy white towels to cover himself when Stefan comes into the bathroom.

'Kenny!'

The older man looks a little dishevelled and smells of red wine and vodka. He isn't his usual scrupulously dapper self. A loosened tie hangs round his open collar, and his jacket hangs open. Clutching the towel round his waist, Kenny bends to gather up his clothes, muttering his apologies for using Stefan's bathroom, before heading for the door.

'Kenny, dear boy, it's OK. You must feel at home here.'

As Kenny moves to go past him, Stefan pats him on the bare shoulder gently, and then unexpectedly leans in to kiss him on the cheek. Kenny panics and pushes him away. As he rushes back to his own room, he can hear Stefan saying, 'So sorry, wrong of me, won't happen again. I promise… Please don't…'

But Kenny, still damp from the bath, is already throwing on his clothes, stuffing his few possessions into his rucksack, and pulling the old sleeping bag down from the top of the wardrobe. Coming out of the room, he sees Stefan sitting on the black-and-white tiled floor. He is crying as Kenny goes into the second bathroom for his toothbrush and sponge bag, which Stefan had given him on his first night here. At the front door, Kenny puts on his warm jacket, feeling the notes for the cab fare still in his pocket, and leaves.

Walking arm in arm along the seafront on Boxing Day, the women squint at the fitful afternoon sun poking between small clouds, their hands stuffed into coat pockets out of reach of the cold, salty wind. Both wear scarves and hats and are quiet, hardly talking, but for an odd word here and there about things they notice, which make them smile – a small child struggling on a bright new bicycle, a man in an over-bright, patterned jumper, probably Christmas presents from the day before. Gemma has been home for a few days now. Glad to be there but still in a state of shock after Bruce's attack. Elizabeth hasn't asked too many questions. Gemma hopes that her mother's not seen the bruising on her neck, hiding underneath the large, soft, knitted scarf she's been wearing since she arrived home, two days earlier than expected. Gemma likes to think that, with the chilly weather, there will be nothing remarkable about her keeping it on in the draughty house.

But Elizabeth has wondered. Wondered not just about the scarf but also about the dark circles under Gemma's eyes, and putting that together with her unexpected arrival, she suspects something is very wrong. She has noticed how Gemma can freeze at the sound of a car's engine in the street, a neighbour's door banging or the telephone ringing. But she is giving it time. Hoping her daughter will open up to her soon. Now, outside and by the sea, thank goodness Gemma seems more relaxed.

They stand for a while looking outwards. The Isle of Wight across the water is hazy today. Sails dot the view, racing along, bending to the wind, and Elizabeth tries to imagine how it would feel out there, tipping over to one side but never quite overbalancing. Is that what her daughter feels right now? Is she desperately trying to keep upright, aware she could lose her stability at any moment?

The wind is getting stronger and after a shared shiver and smile, they turn in the other direction. Elizabeth wants to find something to talk about. The silence has gone on too long.

'Gemma, do you ever wonder what happened to Kenny?'

'Kenny? Of course. Why?'

'Just thinking how you two used to spend every minute of the day with each other.'

'Yes, Mum. Things remind me sometimes. Just coming back into our street. Strange still to see different curtains at his window and that bright red door.'

'No word for poor Sarah after that one postcard. And, remember I found that envelope as well, in the dresser drawer?'

166

'Yes. You know, I've still got the postcard.' Gemma says brightly – inside feeling a shiver as a picture of Bruce sneaks into her head. Bruce by the side of the river in Yorkshire, loudly accusing her of being unfaithful. 'And that old envelope of Sarah's. Wasn't much in it was there? I didn't understand why you seemed so puzzled by it. Just some old black-and-white photos and some wartime cards, you said?'

'The photos, yes. Yes, I was puzzled but then, you know how it is. I didn't think so much at the time, but I keep coming back to it now.' Elizabeth stops for a second, looking out to sea and rebuttoning her coat up to the neck. The wind has got up again. 'I told you how Sarah always said Kenny's dad had drowned. Torpedoed in the Pacific…or was it the Atlantic?'

'Well? And so?'

'It struck me as strange at the time that there weren't any pictures of him. No evidence of a dad at all. Pictures of Kenny as a baby. Pictures of Yvonne, but not even one of her holding the boy. Just strange that's all. Did he ever talk to you about his mum and dad? Sarah kept saying she'd tell him when he was a bit older! I really hope she did.'

'No. And I think I asked him one day. Yes. I do remember now. We must have been still quite little because we were playing hopscotch outside the house, soon after Donald came back. I asked if his dad would be coming back soon. And he just ran off. What are you thinking?'

'Well, I know Sarah always said how Yvonne was going to marry this sailor on his Christmas leave, but the awful telegram about him reached her first. And, of course, there she was, well pregnant, and then, so soon after he was born, she upped and left. But why leave her ration book and identity card? They were in the envelope with the photos. And even if she felt she had to go away, why not at least let her poor mum know where she was living?'

'Well, wasn't it back in 1944, Mum? You've told me often enough about how people just disappeared.'

'She was certainly up in London at some point. Someone had seen her working behind a bar near Piccadilly. But to leave her mum in the dark like that…'

They have passed the pier, and they hesitate, trying to decide whether to go on into the Rock Gardens or head for home. Gemma lifts her head to look straight into Elizabeth's eyes and says, 'Let's go home now, Mum, and have a nice cuppa and one of your mince pies. And I think I'd like a bit of a chat along with it.'

It is somehow still Boxing Day, even though so much has happened since breakfast. The walk in Hyde Park with Stefan, the pause at Speaker's Corner, Stefan meeting his old friend from Warsaw, Kenny's walk back to the flat on his own and his luxurious soaking in Stefan's big bath. Hearing Stefan's key in the door, his appearance in the bathroom and the shock of his kiss.

Kenny still has Stefan's taxi money in his pocket, but he will need that for the train. Doesn't fancy hitch-hiking again. Walking quickly all the way as far as Waterloo Bridge, his head swims. Images – scraps of conversations. With Stefan, Marit, and then from nowhere comes a memory. Granny Sarah lying in bed on that morning, the day he had left. He'd gone up to take her a cup of tea before he went off to work. Why had he only sent her that one card? It was as if he had put all that part of his life into a cupboard and locked the door. As if he had become somebody else, someone disconnected from everything that had gone before.

Sarah had always taken care of him, and she wasn't even his mother. And who was that? What stopped Granny from telling him properly about his parents? She had tried to make out that his father (George, she'd called him) was a hero who had died for his country. But there wasn't a single photo of him anywhere. And Yvonne, his mother? When he was little, he'd not thought about her absence. And then when he was about ten, there'd been that strange conversation. Looking back, he realises it wasn't just him who had felt rather awkward and embarrassed. So had his grandmother. While she spoke to him, she'd been holding her two hands together in that sort of wringing movement he'd seen her do with the wet sheets and towels in the scullery. Not really looking at him as she spoke.

He's reached Waterloo Bridge, and as he starts to walk across the wind bites at his face. Kenny stops halfway across and leans on the wall.

She'll be surprised to see him. Cross with him probably, rightly so, for being away so long. He can't phone. She hasn't got one in the house. It's too late to send a card. How old will she be now?

Staring down at the fast-moving, brownish water, Kenny's eyes focus on the scraps of litter skimming the river's surface. He hardly notices the working boats slowly passing below. He is already thinking of what he'll say to Sarah when he gets back home. Listing in his mind all the questions he wants to ask.

Stefan has told him there are records. Even of people who died in the war. Kenny had known about the stone memorials, great pillars and crosses with names. There was one on Southsea Common near the skating rink, but he'd never gone to look. And, Stefan had said, there were places where you could search for information about people who are still alive. He knew about things like that. He'd done a bit of tracing himself, trying to find details of his own family that he'd left behind in Poland.

He had run away from things too. Stefan. So kind, so clever and helpful. If only he had left him alone. It was the kiss. Not like the kiss from Marit the night they'd arrived at Coldwater Hall. Stefan's kiss was from a kind man who had, up until that moment, made him feel safe. Had made Kenny feel he could become someone. Marit's kiss had felt delicious and like a kind of love at the time, but now he knows it had just been a way of marking him as her possession. An animal act. Not kind. His head feels like it could burst with these contradictions. Marit and Stefan. So different, yet he'd run from both of them.

A seagull wheels past and, folding its wings, sits on the wall a few yards away from Kenny who is, for a moment, back in Stefan's bathroom trying to get the bath sheet to cover his nakedness. And in that instant Stefan was Marit, and Kenny's newly-built feeling of trust had splintered. Like in the *Wizard of Oz* when a curtain is pulled open to reveal a horrible truth. He lifts his eyes to look down the river towards Blackfriars Bridge and St Paul's. The nearby gull lifts off and heads across to the South Bank. It is surprisingly quiet on the bridge. Hardly any traffic. Then Kenny remembers that it is still Boxing Day.

Stefan was crying when he'd left the flat.

Kenny shivers. He thinks he will have to write to him when he gets home. Home? Is that where he is going? How long has he been standing here on the bridge? The sky is fading fast, and lights are coming on all over the place – car headlamps, red warning lights on the tops of cranes, red and green on the craft below. The cold is seeping into him and he should get moving, but his feet seem glued to the pavement. Which way to go if he does move? Back to the flat to see if Stefan is OK? To offer an awkward explanation as a way of saying sorry, to smell onions and garlic and basil cooking on the stove, to sip a glass of Italian red wine? Or on to Waterloo Station to see when there might be a train going to Portsmouth, tonight or tomorrow?

Kenny jumps at the touch of a hand on his shoulder.

'All right, mate? Not thinking of jumping in, are you? Bloody effing cold down there! Not the best time to go for a swim.' Kenny turns and looks into the face that is speaking. The creases of worry round the man's eyes bely the smile and chirpy tone.

Had he been thinking of jumping? No, he thinks not. He was just feeling completely stuck. Didn't know which way to turn his feet.

'It's OK, mate! Just trying to decide something.'

The man's anxious frown grows, and he looks as if he is about to speak again.

'No, not that!' Kenny says, with a quick nod down at the river. 'Don't worry. I'll get on now. Train to catch. But thanks for stopping, for asking. Appreciate it.'

'If you're sure.' The stranger holds out a hand. Kenny feels a little warmth from it as he takes it. The kindness makes him want to cry. But Kenny has never cried easily, unlike Stefan who has talked of it often. Kenny looks once more into the stranger's face, nods, and turns his feet towards Waterloo Station.

They have been out till late afternoon. Shrugging off coats and throwing hats and gloves onto the stand in the hall, Gemma follows her mother into the kitchen. Elizabeth sets the filled kettle on to boil before getting some mince pies from a tin to heat in the oven.

'Can I help, Mum?'

'Get that gas fire lit in the front room, Gem, and put on the lamps.'

Gemma kneels by the fire. Hearing the spark light the gas, she stays down for a second or two, until the elements begin to glow. Holding out a hand to feel the heat, she stays, staring at the growing brightness, lost in thought until she hears Elizabeth call.

'Come on, Gemma love, come and get this tray for me and I'll bring the rest. I'm dying for my cuppa.'

Back in the kitchen, the smell of the warming mincemeat and pastry brings back childhood Christmas memories. Tea parties on Christmas Eve, decorating the tiny tree with bits and pieces collected over the years, Elizabeth all dusty with pastry flour, Sarah and Kenny coming over with an iced cake, and some small, wrapped things. Never anything expensive, often hand-made. Kenny grinning at her in excitement. A knitted scarf. A jar of chutney. A box of crackers. How simple life was then.

Gemma takes the tray laden and rattling with the cups, saucers, and plates and sets it down on the coffee table. She sits in the armchair nearest the fire. Then hears her mother going upstairs. The sound of a drawer opening and shutting.

When Elizabeth brings in the tea and mince pies, she looks at her daughter who is staring into space, still wearing the big woollen scarf round her neck. Elizabeth pours the tea with a half-anxious eye on Gemma.

'Here, Gem love, take one of these,' she says quietly, handing her a holly-leaf paper napkin with the tea. 'And take a mince pie. I'm not sure if the mincemeat is as good as last year's, but eat it up quick while it's still warm.' Under her arm, Elizabeth is holding a very old-looking large brown envelope.

'What's that you've got there, Mum?'

'Something I've had a long, long time, Gemma love. And I've decided to get it out from my drawer now, because we were talking about Kenny, remember? And I was saying how his mum disappeared. You remember when Sarah died, and you came home for the funeral?'

'Of course, Mum. And you helped to clear the house. And found the card from Kenny.'

'Yes, I did. And that's when I also found this envelope. I'm sorry now that I never talked it over with you then. At the time it felt so private and, like I said this afternoon, I didn't know quite what to think about it. Then soon after, you went back to Birmingham, and Kenny was goodness knows where. And who was there to tell? So, I'm going to tell you now...'

When Elizabeth had done all she could for Sarah's little house, she took a last look around the kitchen, double-checking the drawers in the big wall dresser. Straightening the lining paper in one drawer, she found the old postcard from Kenny. She remembered Sarah telling her about it at the time, but she hadn't seen the card. Sarah had started to get tearful and upset, so Elizabeth had let it go. In the other drawer, where the knife box had been, was a large envelope. Gently drawing it towards her, she had a momentary sense of Sarah looking over her shoulder. Would Sarah want her to look inside? How private were the contents?

Taking her discovery to the window by the sink, Elizabeth turned the envelope over in her hands. It was addressed to Sarah and the postmark was some-time in 1945. She could see the curled edge of a few photographs along with some official-looking cards.

Still questioning herself, she paused, wanting to hear or at least feel, Sarah's permission for the next step.

Pulling out the contents, she laid everything out on the draining board. First the photographs. Yvonne as a chubby baby, lying on her front on a rug, laughing up at the camera. Yvonne as a very young woman, looking slightly awkward, with a bleak smile. No picture of a laughing, handsome sailor on leave with an arm round her waist, then. No picture of Yvonne smiling down at her new born boy. Just the one picture outside the church after Kenny's christening. There they were on the steps of the church, Sarah holding the white bundle that was Kenny, Yvonne looking blankly ahead, a couple of other neighbours. It was only a few weeks later that Yvonne had gone away – had just disappeared. Elizabeth did remember that day of the christening. She had moved into the street a few months before, already pregnant with Gemma. Donald somewhere far away. Sarah, being neighbourly, had invited her to the church event. A few days later, over a cup of tea, Sarah had told her how Yvonne's fiancé had gone down with his ship. How they'd planned to marry at Christmas, but the telegram reached her daughter before any Christmas cards.

After Yvonne had gone, Sarah made out that it was all part of a plan. Yvonne was going to get a job in London, and when she was settled, she would send for Kenny. Perhaps Sarah believed that, but Elizabeth always had her doubts. As the months passed, and there was no word from Yvonne, both women gradually stopped mentioning her. But Elizabeth knew, as the years went by, that Sarah was left with the question of what to tell Kenny.

Then she turned to touch, one at a time, the faded official cards. The blue identity document with Yvonne's name and address inside and her green nursing-mother's ration book, and a post office savings book with a balance of one shilling and sixpence. Holding these scraps in her hand, her thoughts began to tidy themselves into a different picture of the past. A picture that said Yvonne had wanted to disappear. Otherwise, why had she left, taking nothing with her? Not one of her documents. And not her baby son.

Elizabeth put everything back in the envelope carefully, slipped it into her bag with Kenny's postcard, and left the house, locking up and pocketing the key ready to pass on to the landlord.

'Gosh, Mum. Oh, poor Sarah. And poor Kenny. He said she'd told him one day when he'd asked – he'd always had questions, but it took him years to ask her – she'd said his dad was a hero in the navy and died in the war, and after that his mum had had to do important war work somewhere in the north. And then he'd stopped asking because Granny Sarah always looked so upset when he did. He said he couldn't bear it when she got upset.'

'I expect Kenny is still asking himself questions, even now.' Elizabeth leans forward to top up Gemma's tea. 'And what about you, my love? Do you ever think about your dad?'

'Not a lot, Mum, to be honest. I'm curious, I suppose. But he was just a stranger when he turned up. And, to be truthful, I never stopped thinking of him as a stranger. He was Donald,

175

never Dad, really. And then you explained that he had a job a long way away and that he wouldn't be back. And you didn't seem sad or upset, so that seemed to be that.'

'You haven't missed having a dad?'

'Hard to say. Yes and no. And you... Haven't you missed having a man around?'

'Hmm.' Elizabeth looks into her teacup for a moment, unsure how to answer her daughter. 'They're not all they're cracked up to be, Gem. Women can manage perfectly well without them, you know.' She smiles, looking up at Gemma. 'Well, with a bit of common sense and a lot of luck. Anyway, what about your Bruce? Will you be managing without him?'

There's an awkward silence between them, which seems to go on and on. They both try a few more sips of tea, and push a few pastry crumbs about a plate to fill the gap, but the tea is getting cold now, and any remaining mincemeat has stuck to the plates. Elizabeth doesn't want to push her daughter. But there's something wrong. She could ask more questions, but whatever it is, maybe it's better coming from her. Then Gemma takes off the scarf and lays it on the arm of the chair. And bursts into tears.

'Oh, my God!' Elizabeth sighs and reaches a hand to touch Gemma lightly on a wet cheek.

'Mum, I'm so sorry.'

They both listen to the hiss of the gas fire, wondering how to safely say what is in their minds.

'Jesus Christ, Gemma, if someone has hurt you, which clearly they have, I'm not wanting to hear any apologies. Just tell me what happened.' Gemma is looking back at the gas fire. 'Well? Was it something in the street? God knows I've worried myself to bits about you living so far away in a big city.'

'No, Mum. I knew you'd say that. I wasn't mugged up in the big bad city, and I wasn't burgled.' She's crying again. 'It was Bruce!' As she says his name, her chest heaves and she struggles to breathe through the sobs. Elizabeth goes quickly to sit on the arm of the chair and puts her arms around Gemma's shoulders, then lifts a hand to gently stroke her hair back off her damp forehead.

'OK, now listen to me, my girl. First, I'm going to get each of us a large glass of Christmas sherry, and then, if you don't mind, I want you to start at the beginning.'

Sipping her sherry rather more quickly than usual, Elizabeth is trying to digest the story. She has met Bruce the boyfriend. Has enjoyed talking to Bruce, the polite young man, the attentive and helpful support for her daughter, the assiduous student. And now here is Bruce the bully, the jealous persecutor, full of intrusive questioning and unjustified accusations of infidelity. Chameleon Bruce, switching in a moment into the heartfelt apologiser, the bearer of flowers. Until finally he loses control. Bruce the attacker. Able to hurt without caring.

'I'm so sorry, Mum.'

'Stop. Gemma, don't you dare apologise to me again.' Elizabeth gets up. For a moment her nervous energy takes her to the dresser to tidy an already neat row of books, to shift an ornamental china shepherdess an infinitesimal distance to the left, and then back to where it was. Sitting back on her chair, she starts again. 'Now let me get this straight. You'd broken it off with Bruce before this? And then you went back to him?'

'Yes.'

'Why the hell did you do that?'

Gemma takes a big breath. Frowns, looks down at the hands fidgeting in her lap.

'OK. Remember I told you how I wanted to move in with some friends, and to get away from the old landlady's busy-bodying? Well, it was actually just after the big row I'd had with Bruce in Yorkshire. And that went fine except that Bruce found out where I was living. I bet bloody Beryl told him the address. And he turned up out of the blue one weekend when the others had gone away. I was having a bit of a bad time. Sometimes I get this thing...'

Gemma looks up to see her mother's face seeming to echo something of her own confusion. The gas fire hisses into the silence until Gemma gathers her thoughts and starts again. 'I'm not like you, Mum. Not so good all on my own, don't know why, and so when he...he arrived with the flowers and the wine and the apologies and all his, "now I realise why you were so upset", and his, "I understand and that will never happen again", and the "how can you forgive me?" and "I've been in such misery thinking I'd lost the best thing that's ever happened to me," and so on... He made me feel sorry for him. Fucking sorry for him! How the fuck did that happen? Sorry, Mum. For swearing I mean.'

The two of them sit in silence again, thinking. A car drives fast up the street and stops outside, and Gemma freezes. A car door slams. Her eyes meet her mother's. Elizabeth quickly moves to the window, peers out between the curtains and comes back to reassure her.

'It's just the new neighbours going into Sarah's old place. They're just back from somewhere. It's OK. Go on.'

Gemma is breathing again. 'After that visit, after he went back to London last month, he's been writing, sending funny cards and messages.' She's crying again. 'He kept asking me to call him from the student union every few days, getting cross if I missed a day. And I wanted to think it was going to be OK.

The plan was that he'd visit at the end of term for a couple of nights before I was coming down here. But whenever I called him, he started saying that I should, *must* go with him down to his parents for Christmas instead of here, and I just kept saying no. I hated the way he wouldn't leave it. And then, I could hear it on the phone, I realised how much he was drinking. He wasn't like that when I first met him. But in the pub in Yorkshire, I'd started to notice it. And then—' Gemma's head is down. Her hands have covered her eyes for a moment.

'And then?' asks Elizabeth, reaching over to top up the sherry in Gemma's glass.

'Then, when he arrived a day early, I just knew. Knew it was going to blow up. He was already in the house cooking…already smelled of drink, and I thought, if I tried to say the right things, not to provoke him, we might get through the evening OK and I could leave early the next day, maybe pretend you were ill or something. He kept on with the wine while he was cooking, and he didn't stop – with the wine or with the questions. Why wasn't I going to come with him to his parents? Why was I coming back here? Was I meeting someone here? Was it the man he'd seen me with near the library?' Elizabeth looks puzzled. 'Yes, he'd arrived in the afternoon, it seems, and gone to look for me at the university. He'd seen me talking to my tutor from a distance, said nothing to me, and then started with the accusations after a bottle of wine. I hadn't even known he was there, for God's sake. That got me really scared. Can you imagine it? He'd just stood there, watching us. So creepy.'

Gemma's voice has been gradually rising, and she's now almost shouting. Better angry than apologetic, thinks Elizabeth. 'I was scared, Mum! I tried really hard to be calm and keep him calm, and guess what? It didn't work. Then this,' and she puts a hand to her bruised neck.

Elizabeth is silent. She is shaken. She knows what Gemma is talking about.

'Listen to me, Gem. You're a grown woman now, and I need to tell you something.' She shuts her eyes for a moment. 'I've met men like Bruce before. During the war, while your dad was away. Men who were all politeness, presents and flattery at the start of an evening until they'd had a few beers. I never got into any big trouble, never got hurt like you, but looking back now, there were some pretty close shaves.'

'What? Mum, you've never said this before.'

'Look, some of it was because I felt alone, missing your dad, not knowing if I'd see him again. I knew friends, girls I'd been to school with, who were widows by their early twenties.'

'I've always had you down as so strong. The way you've always talked…going through the bombing and everything and always coping. Hard to imagine you being as stupid as me.'

They look at each other and almost smile. Elizabeth shakes her head a little as she examines her daughter's face. Wonders how much to tell her.

'So, now what? What do you want to happen next?'

'Just don't know, Mum, except I don't want him anywhere near me ever again. Promise me, you'll never let him in, or tell him where I am.'

Elizabeth is sitting alone by the gas fire, staring at the glowing elements. Gemma has gone to bed. She has tucked her daughter in, just as she used to when she was little, leaving a mug of sweetened cocoa by her side.

She finds herself thinking again about Yvonne. People in the street had told her how Yvonne was always such a happy child, and a cheerful young woman, even with the war going on. Then suddenly she had changed. Just before she was seen to be pregnant. Elizabeth wonders, why no photos of a fiancé? No one in the street had apparently set eyes on him. And there was always that slight sense that Sarah was keeping something back. Something she couldn't tell Elizabeth. Or Kenny. And Yvonne couldn't bear to stay with her baby son. Perhaps Sarah hadn't been able to keep her daughter safe, just as Elizabeth has failed to do with hers.

Kenny's spirits sink even lower when, after climbing the steps and going through Waterloo's great Victory Arch, he finds that he has missed the last train to Portsmouth. It's still Boxing Day, so of course there has been a reduced service, and he must wait until the early morning. Sitting on the concrete floor near the toilets, his back against a wall, he shivers, even with his sleeping bag wrapped round his shoulders. The toilets send out their strong urinary message to any passer-by, competing with an unkind dank wind breathing its way in intermittent gusts through the concourse. The crash of the metal grilles on the platforms as they open and shut puncture his dreams – he is back in the state he was in before Stefan, vigilant to the sound of footsteps. Some station official comes over to look at him. The man's laced shoes seem huge, appearing close to Kenny's slowly opening eyes. The man's brusque questions seem to reach Kenny's ears from somewhere in the dark shadows above. Kenny pulls out Stefan's pound notes from his jacket pocket to show the man that he has money for a ticket so is not just a bum, and the shoes and questions retreat.

Hours pass, footsteps are rarer, any voices are sporadic and lack clarity. The great space of the station around Kenny has a distorting effect on any sound. Drifting back into sleep, he is first back in his old spot under the railway arches near the river, then back in Stefan's kitchen watching him chop onions and tomatoes, and sprinkle green basil leaves into a pan. But Stefan's face is suddenly contorted with anger. Kenny surfaces from the dream suddenly after seeing Stefan again, crying, bent over, crumpled into himself on the hall carpet.

When a pigeon flaps past quite close, before soaring up to perch on a roof beam, Kenny is back in the present, aware that he has heard a station announcement. A woman's voice, but the words are indecipherable. Raising his head slightly, he watches the pigeon, thinks it is surveying the whole place while deciding where to go next – as he had stood, still and undecided on Waterloo Bridge. Had that concerned stranger helped him decide?

A very pale light is reaching its fingers through the beams, and Kenny, thankful that a new day has arrived, starts to move his stiffened arms and legs. He feels like one of those tightly jointed wooden toys he played with years ago. He pictures needing a puppeteer to hold him up by strings to straighten out his locked limbs. Waterloo Station is waking up around him. Once he's standing up, Kenny walks around a bit, trying to loosen his joints. It had been evening when he'd arrived, so once he'd made sure there were no trains to Portsmouth till morning, he'd found his place of rest. There'd been no space on any of the benches. Now he looks about, getting his bearings. There's the gents, there's the ticket office, over there a WH Smiths, there's a café of some kind, still closed, although he hears the chinking of china, and a faint light shows through from behind the shutters.

A sudden clatter of boards behind him draws his attention to the enormous information display. The clattering is continuing as place names appear, disappear and reappear as if they too are trying to make up their minds. His neck feels stiff as he looks up to search for what he needs. A train to Portsmouth Harbour. And he finds it, feeling a rush of something that is a mixture of relief and uncertainty. Yes, he can get home. But what then? He stands, trying to do the sums – how long he has been away? How old was Granny Sarah then, and what will that make her now? Leaving the questions for later, he heads for the ticket office and after queuing for ten minutes, buys his ticket. A single.

'Are you sure, lad? Cheaper to get a return in the long run,' the ticket man had said.

Kenny hadn't replied, other than a shake of his head, before taking the ticket. He cannot imagine coming back – can only think about getting there.

Lights are coming on all over the station and, although it is still early, the space is beginning to fill with people intent on finding a route round each other, or standing, as he had been, craning heads up to find the name they seek on the high boards. Men in bowler hats, in flat caps, women in tiny hats with flowers and lace, boys in school uniform, young lads in sailors' bell bottoms – a throng coming away from platforms, dodging or impatiently pushing into a crowd heading toward the trains, newspapers under arms, rolled umbrellas and briefcases, handbags, naval kitbags, and Christmas parcels. Kenny finds his platform, shows his ticket to the collector at the gate and is soon seated by a window, clutching his rucksack on his lap and rolling the sleeping bag under his knees.

The Day After Boxing Day

Gemma wakes from an unusually deep sleep. Was it the relief of talking, the comfort of her mother's presence the night before? The way Elizabeth had remained sitting on the bed, like when she was a child, stroking her hair, watching her drift off after the sweetened cocoa.

Gemma tries to guess the time. It is late December. The light coming through the faded curtains must mean that it is at least nine o'clock, or even later. She can hear movement in the room below so her mother is up already. What will she be thinking about after all of last night's conversations and revelations? There is enough light now to let her look around the room. She realises she has avoided doing this until now. Arriving in an almost catatonic state before Christmas, she'd hardly noticed her surroundings – had been just glad to be back in a safe place. She'd not even properly unpacked yet.

Had just thrown a few things onto the old wicker chair. She'd been keenly aware of any noises outside the house. A car in the street. A knock on a door. A man's footsteps. But felt unable to focus on anything nearer so hadn't taken in the signs of another person's occupancy.

Audrey, the student who rents this room in term time, has gone home for Christmas. Uncomfortably, there are framed photographs on the dressing table of Audrey's family. Strangers. Looking for other clues, Gemma sees an unfamiliar brush and comb sitting next to the mirror. A few threads of dark hair cling to the bristles. So she is dark haired. And clearly not too fussy. The badly sellotaped posters on the wall tell Gemma that the student likes the Beatles. And Picasso. Some art books on a shelf, next to some of Gemma's childhood books, remind her that the girl is an art student. She ponders this evidence of a stranger's presence before she drifts off to sleep again.

Gemma doesn't hear the knock on the door over the road. If she had looked out of the window a little earlier, she might have seen a dishevelled young man talking to the woman in the wrap-around apron in the doorway, two small children clinging round her knees. She might have noticed the hand the woman had brought to her mouth, to the other hand then placed gently on the young man's shoulder. Might have seen the back of the young man running back down the road, carrying a sleeping bag and rucksack.

After turning into the street, eager for the safety of his old home, Kenny thought at first that he must have come to the wrong house. The front door, remembered by him as a peeling grey, was now a shiny red. Instead of the familiar old knocker, a fancy brass one hung there, shaped like a lion's paw. Looking for the usual greying nets at the upper windows, he found instead floral-patterned blinds.

Wanting to hear Sarah's voice, longing, now he was back here, for her to look at him with her old eyes. Kenny rapped with the lion's paw – for a moment, nothing – then footsteps and some scurrying and small voices. When the door opened, he stared. A woman of about thirty, he guessed, was tussling with two small children competing to be picked up. The woman's smile disappeared as he stared at her.

'Yes, what can I do for you?' she asked.

He could smell coffee. He smelled toast and in spite of himself, his mouth watered. After a longer moment of staring, as Kenny tried to gather his wits, he said, 'My granny. Sarah. Where is she?'

The woman's hand flew to her mouth.

'Sarah? Oh my God. You're her grandson, aren't you? Oh, sweetheart, didn't you know? She's gone. Last summer.' The woman put out her other hand on his shoulder.

'Gone where?' But he began to guess. Wanted this woman to go back inside and shut the door and not tell him. But she was still there and was calling back down the hallway.

'Fred, I need you. Come quick and get these two monsters please.'

A man in shirtsleeves and corduroy trousers came out and nodded to Kenny, before picking up the children, one in each arm and retreating.

'Oh, you poor lamb, you didn't know. Darling, I'm afraid Sarah died. Last July, I think. We moved in soon after they cleared the house. Look, please come inside. You've gone white as a sheet. Let me get you a cup of tea. And some toast. You look half-starved.'

But Kenny had already turned and started to run. He didn't want to know. Couldn't bear to hear anymore. All his apologies now never to be heard. No chance to explain. No chance to ask. All his questions, never to be answered.

He didn't stop running until he reached the seafront. And there was the old seaside shelter. Where he'd sat while Marit had poured all that sweetness into his ears. There she'd sat, talking in that not-quite-English way of hers, about how she loved beautiful things, how she had travelled all over Europe, how she knew about a wider world than his own. His small world where the most excitement was having enough coins to hire skating boots at the rink. Or affording a packet of Woodbines. Marit's voice had stirred that powerful longing in him for more than that. To see somewhere else. To be somewhere different. And also, as she'd gazed into his eyes and placed a soft sweet-smelling hand over his knee, an excitement for things he didn't yet know about in his head, but which he could magically imagine in his body.

Approaching the shelter, he was aware of his absolute exhaustion. It was still early and there were very few people about. A short fat woman was walking a large, ugly and hairless dog towards the pier. A young couple walked by the edge of the water holding hands, oblivious to him or anyone else. A frail, white-haired couple were strolling towards the Rock Garden's entrance, arms laced tight as if holding each other up.

Kenny spread out his sleeping bag on the bench inside the shelter – where he'd sat and listened to Marit offering him a place on her grand estate. He longed to lie back and sleep, with the sound of the waves in his ears. To not think any more. He crawled into the sleeping bag and, pulling a jumper out of his sack, made a pillow out it. Stefan's Christmas-present. And holding his rucksack tight to his chest, Kenny first wept a little then slept.

Elizabeth is outside pegging out the washed sheets in the December sunshine. She has already peeked in at Gemma and been relieved to see her still sleeping, mouth open slightly, the remains of last night's cocoa smearing the mug on the bedside table. She decides to leave her to lie-in. She used to love watching her sleep when she was little. Used to creep up like this, just to make sure.

Elizabeth stretches up with the last peg. Not so easy to do this. I'm not getting any younger, she thinks.

A plastic-covered line now, not like the old rope one.

She needs her rest, after last night. They learned a lot about each other. The sherry had made it go quicker, maybe, but not sure about having said so much. Even after all these years thinking again about those times. Feeling so alone, so wanting to dance, longing to be held, to be appreciated.

She stands for a moment after putting the empty basket under one arm, seeing the images again of uniforms, banks of musicians, a shiny floor – colourful, if skimpy dresses.

She hadn't told Gemma the whole story, of course, she thought as she walked quickly to the corner shop for fresh bread and milk. No need.

Back in the kitchen, there is still no sign of Gemma, until Elizabeth spots the scribbled note under the teapot, and the rinsed cup upside down at the side of the sink:

Need fresh air, Mum. Off to smell the sea. Thanks for cocoa and helpful chat last night. Slept like a dream. Gemma xxx

Elizabeth hadn't slept well. Shocked by Gemma's revelations and, stirred by her own memories dislodged from under a stone by the signs of Bruce's violence on Gemma's neck, she is relieved now to feel the emptiness of the house. Glad of the time to get to grips with the turbulence that had disturbed her sleep.

Reaching a hand out to the kettle, she feels the warmth. So, she's not been gone long. After refilling it, she lights a gas ring and, holding the kettle in one hand, stares at the orange-blue flames, before lowering it onto the heat. Why is it so hard to decide if she wants tea or coffee? Not sure which mug to use. Not sure if she can bear to know more about Gemma's time in Birmingham. Not sure if she wants her daughter to know more about her own wartime entanglements. Not much different from millions of others, dreading the bombs, not knowing if you'd be there the next day, men fighting who-knew-where, telegrams arriving at doors you knew... Well, the music and the dancing did help and so did the attention from those poor chaps between one terrifying battle and another. Better to pull the cover right back over the whole damn thing.

Elizabeth stretches up to get a very old blue and white china cup from its hook. Where did that one come from? Surely, it's been here in this house as long as I have. And then it comes to her. Donald had won it for her, knocking a coconut off its perch – must have been way back in '39, at a fair on Southsea Common. Donald! What on earth happened to him? Dead or alive? With someone or on his own? Another family? If he's alive, does he ever think of her, or of Gemma? Strange thing when someone from years back pops into your head, and then you wonder if you are ever in their minds in any way. Or maybe never.

Looking down, she notices that the decorated tin of tea leaves is in one of her hands, the measuring spoon in the other, although she doesn't remember how they got there. She watches her own hands with interest as she spoons the tea. Such a familiar action. How many times have I made tea for myself since being in this house? What a daft question. And tea for Donald? Not so many times. He wasn't here much during the war and gone before you could say Jack Robinson after he got himself back from Hamburg and into his demob suit. She hears the kettle boiling. As she pours the steaming water into the pot and puts the lid on, time seems to have slowed right down. Elizabeth discovers that she has already sat down on her usual chair, elbows on the table, hands to her chin.

Since she went off to college, Gemma's only here a few weeks of the year. Audrey, the lodger is only here in term time. Anyway, she drinks coffee. And not your Nescafé instant. She makes real coffee in a fancy jug and filter that she brought with her. It smells good, but when Elizabeth's occasionally drunk a cup, it's been too strong. And Sarah. How many pots of tea shared in this house and over the road?

Glancing down, Elizabeth wonders how she has a hanky in her hand. Had she found it in her apron pocket? Feeling tears on her cheeks, she wipes her face quickly in surprise. Trying to feel more normal, she pours tea into the cup and adds milk. Looking up, Sarah's old green cake tin catches her eye. Just broken biscuits in there now. What she'd give for Sarah to walk through the door right now, holding the tin in front of her, with its smell of iced sponge buns or fruit cake. Poor, dear thing. First Yvonne leaves a note on the table and her son in his cot and went away – who knew where? Then Kenny, off up north to a fancy job somewhere. One postcard and that was it. Then Sarah, hardly complaining, but slipping away from life with a cough and a fever. And all that's left is a cake tin and…and, of course, Yvonne's papers. Kept at the back of a kitchen drawer by Sarah for all those years. Now in Elizabeth's bedroom chest of drawers again.

While Elizabeth is sipping her tea, Gemma is walking briskly towards the seafront, her mind far away from the present. On the way, she stops and sits in the Rock Gardens. Choosing a bench near the fountain, childhood memories flood through her. When she was little, she and Kenny had been allowed to stay up late one night each August to walk along the promenade, entranced by the strings of coloured lights hanging between lamp posts, to see the illuminations and firework display from the end of the pier. Part of the annual treat had been to walk through the Rock Gardens in the dark. She'd been hypnotised every year by the light display, which kept changing the colour of the water in the fountain, spilling out to light up the exotic vegetation round the edge of the little pond below. Everyone walking along nearby had seemed so much bigger. Kenny and Sarah used to come too. Kenny on one side of her, Mum on the other, Sarah holding one of Kenny's hands tight, anxious about losing him in the crowd, because she had nearly lost him once, on a hot day near the beach, and they'd all rushed around in a panic till Elizabeth had spotted him, in tears. When the fireworks began, she and Kenny would be oohing and aahing in unison at the starbursts from the rockets, jumping up together at the bangers and crackers, clutching each other when the final display spread its light and noise across the sky. The effect doubled by its reflection in the water below. The children would have been made to have an afternoon nap so they could manage the late night, but their feet would still be dragging along with tiredness by the time they were all back in their street.

Coming back into the present, Gemma raises herself off the bench and heads towards the sound of the sea. Reaching the promenade, she stands for a while watching and listening to the ebb and flow of the waves. She might have gone to sit in the old shelter, but it looks like someone is sleeping there. A tramp maybe, sleeping off too much cider? Common enough on the streets of Birmingham. Instead, she steps down onto the beach, treading carefully on the pebbles until she is at the water's edge. The Isle of Wight is shrouded in mist but still visible. She finds herself thinking about all the talking last night…about bullies who begin by being Prince Charming and end up more like Bluebeard. She'd been shocked by some of her mother's wartime revelations, but it seemed to help Elizabeth understand what had been going on with Bruce.

Now she isn't sure she wants to know any more. When you have new knowledge, new images, you have to readjust your old picture frames, and she realises that isn't easy. She is scanning the sea now, counting all the small yachts as they skim behind and in front of the historic fort. Farther out she can see the foamy trail of a power boat as it crosses the path of the car ferry that is making its way to Ryde.

A chill is slowly creeping over her. How long has she been here, staring out to sea? Looking at her watch, Gemma knows she wants to go home to see her mother, to make sure she is still the same person, the one that she is used to keeping as a comfort in her mind.

Turning away from the sea, she retraces her steps through the Rock Gardens, not noticing the young man with a sleeping bag under one arm, who is heading off in a hurry along the promenade in the direction of the pier.

*

Hearing the cry of the gulls overhead, Kenny thought about opening his eyes, as he tried to pull himself out of his vivid dreams. It took him a moment or two to register where he was. Marit's? No musky perfume; no imperious demands. Under the arches in London? No footsteps, no smell of piss. Stefan's? No sizzle of meat in a frying pan, no aroma of pasta sauce, deliciously mixed with cigar smoke and aftershave. Waterloo Station? No, the cries were of gulls, not pigeons. No loud but inaudible announcements. Opening his eyes at last, he stared up at the clouds drifting across a blue sky and thought for a second that he could hear the sound of milk being poured over Rice Krispies. Then recognised it as the sound of foamy water running back and forth over the loose pebbles at the shoreline.

The shore, where he and Gemma would be allowed to take off socks and sandals and paddle. Where they'd stand clinging to each other and squealing with excitement at the cold and the movement of the waves. How old was he when he knew he could stay afloat in the water? Gemma had learned before him, and he had felt jealous, although it wouldn't have been a word he'd have known back then. Gemma's mum was a good swimmer and had often carried her out to deep water so she wouldn't ever fear it. His granny hadn't ever swum and was always afraid. She'd sit on her beach blanket by the water's edge, her worried frown following him closely as the water lapped his knees, a bird-like small cry escaping her if he ventured further, a louder gasp if he let himself get caught by a sudden wave.

And his own mother? He can now at least say these words – can ask himself this question, realising that he had been hanging onto a bit of hope, all the way from Waterloo on the early morning train. An idea that his mother's mother would give him some answers. That Sarah would release some truth she'd been unable to share when he was a boy. Stunned at the news of her death, he felt as if a huge wooden door had slammed shut, any answers about his origins lost in the fog of war, as Stefan would often say. Kenny turned on his side to look out to sea. Watched the gulls landing, taking off, soaring and circling. Stefan had told him how he'd known men who had lost limbs in the war and thought they could still feel the absent leg or arm like a phantom that wouldn't ever go away. Kenny's questions about his beginnings felt like that. No answers now but the curiosity still following him around like a desperately hungry but hopeful cat.

Kenny rolled off the bench onto his feet. It took him a moment to get his balance before stretching his arms wide, lifting his face up to the weak sun. His empty stomach called out for attention. He knew he was grubby and smelled slightly rank. He'd got so used to these things when he was on the London pavements, he'd quickly ceased to notice, but since being at Stefan's, he knew what it felt like to be clean and well fed. Looking in the direction of the pier, he remembered using the gents there, years ago. He still had a bit of change from the train fare in a pocket. Rolling up the sleeping bag and hoisting the rucksack over one shoulder, he headed off along the promenade, eager to wash his face and hands, clean his teeth and use the toilet. After that, maybe he would see a cheap place to get a bun and a cup of something warm.

There were not many people about. It was too cold for most, apart from a few dog walkers. Halfway along, passing the entrance to the Rock Gardens, he caught sight of a young woman, a brightly coloured thick scarf wrapped round her head and neck, disappearing down the shallow stone steps that led to the fountain. Something vaguely familiar? But maybe it was just the scarf. Not quite like Marit's and the girl didn't move at all like her.

Loneliness hit him suddenly like a hailstorm that you can't avoid. That stings. That hurts. He walked more quickly now towards the old pier, elegantly white against the blue sky.

In the pier toilets, Kenny splashed his face again and again with the clean water. Looking up at the mirror, for a second didn't recognise himself. Exhaustion and hunger were slowing down his thinking. Was this the same face that he'd seen in Stefan's mirror when he tried on the Christmas-present jumper? Then the unexpected sight of Stefan's face behind him, Stefan's face watching him, with a warm glow about his eyes. Kenny remembered something similar with Marit, her face in the giant mirror at Coldwater Hall that first night. Today, he saw in front of him a young man with the saddest of eyes, with wet strands of hair flopping down over an unsmiling face. No one behind him this time. Just a painted brick wall with an old curling poster advertising an event that had already been and gone. Kenny's feet felt stuck to the floor with indecision, as they had been on Waterloo Bridge yesterday. Was it only yesterday?

When an older man entered the room behind him to use the urinal, Kenny moved quickly towards the door. His streetwise vigilance hadn't left him, and he was back out on the promenade in a flash. As he was queuing to get a tea and a bun at a small kiosk, the image of the young woman he'd seen earlier nudged at his mind, and it came to him that she reminded him of Gemma. Gemma, who'd still been at school when he'd last set eyes on her. He wondered where she was now. College probably, he'd said to Stefan when he had asked. And her mother, Elizabeth. Might she have moved away? Or even died? As he took the cup of tea and the bun wrapped in a napkin, intending to sit on a nearby bench, he was hit by a longing for someone familiar who knew him, knew him before Marit, before Stefan. Someone who knows, knew, Sarah. Even someone who knew Sarah before he was born and would remember his parents, who might know where his mother went, and why. He felt sure now that Sarah's story, told when he was only ten, was just that – a story. He hadn't wanted to know, hadn't wanted to think about it then, and now she was gone.

In a sudden move, Kenny placed the china cup noisily back on the counter, its saucer swimming with the remaining cold tea, and threw the sticky napkin into the nearby bin. Then he was striding away from the seafront, back towards his old street. He wondered if Elizabeth's door would be the same colour, unsure if he would dare to knock for fear of a crushing disappointment.

Back home, Gemma hung her coat in the hall. She still wore the scarf round her neck and shoulders, in spite of no longer needing to keep her bruises secret. Her mother's voice came to her from the kitchen.

'Darling, you're back. I bet you're starving as well as cold. Scrambled egg on toast and some beans? How will that be?'

'Just the thing, Mum. I'll just pop up and wash my hands, and I'll be ready for it.' There was a pause before Gemma took to the stairs. Her voice sounded a little unnatural as she called out. 'No messages, Mum? No one's phoned?'

Elizabeth appeared at the kitchen door.

'No, love. I know what you're thinking. But I'm sure he'll be at his parents, drowning his sorrows or whatever.'

'But Mum, he might drive over—'

'Stop that, Gemma. He must have got the message.

Anyway, he wouldn't dare show his face here after what he did to you. Put him out of your mind and get yourself back down here sharpish before your eggs get cold. And I'm making you some of that fancy coffee from Audrey's stores!'

Elizabeth, stirring the eggs and butter slowly, wished she could reassure Gemma that there'd be no more from Bruce. Wished she could believe it herself.

Sitting at the table, they were just finishing their plates of food when there was a knock at the door. Gemma froze, a fork halfway to her mouth. Stared at Elizabeth.

'Don't answer it, Mum.'

Elizabeth stood and reached over the table to put her arms round her daughter's shoulders. Breathed quietly over the top of her head.

'It's probably not him, love. But if you want to, go upstairs quietly into your room, while I go and have a look out of the bay window and take a peek to see who it is. I promise, *promise*, I won't let him in – if it is him, which it probably isn't.'

Elizabeth's door had been repainted, but it was the same colour that Kenny remembered from childhood. There was no fancy new knocker, and there was a plant pot he recognised on the ledge of the tiny hall window. He rattled the old letterbox tentatively and waited. In the silence, his heart was beating nineteen to the dozen. A car horn blared from the next street, clearly going too fast. Then he heard footsteps in the house, and managed to control the urge to run. His hand was reaching forward, about to try one more knock, when Elizabeth opened the door. It only took her a second to recognise him.

'Kenny. Oh, for goodness sake, Kenny love.' And she had her arms round him before she'd got the words out.

A sob escaped him, and then he couldn't stop crying as she held him tighter. His head was buried in her shoulder so he didn't notice the footsteps running down the stairs. But then heard a voice…one so familiar that it seemed to have lived forever in his bones.

'Kenny. Oh my God. Is it really you?'

He looked up and past Elizabeth to the girl standing behind her. The girl with the big scarf. The girl he'd seen by the sea.

Kenny lies in the warm bath, upstairs in this still-familiar place. Wonders if he is dreaming.

The house feels so much smaller than he remembers. As he'd come up the little staircase, he'd felt clumsily too big for it, as if he had taken a bite from Alice in Wonderland's EAT ME cake and had suddenly grown into a giant. Raising himself slowly out of water that smells of Palmolive soap, it is a joy to feel clean again. Drying his body with the big green towel, he hears noises from the kitchen downstairs. Faint voices but no words. He feels suddenly wary. Last time he had a bath, Stefan had come in and he'd had to grab a towel to hide himself. There are no footsteps on the stairs, so he relaxes a little but wonders what the voices are saying about him.

When they had all met, just an hour ago on the doorstep, he had heard himself apologising through his sudden tears, saying he couldn't come in, was too grubby, stinking, just wanted to ask them if…if they knew about… But Mrs Siddons had insisted that he get himself inside, with his sleeping bag and rucksack, and to sit down, and if it helped him to feel comfortable, if he was really worried, then she would run him a bath and make him some breakfast and after that they could all talk, because she didn't want him going anywhere right now. 'We have all day, Kenny,' she'd said. 'And you've been away so long. And now you are such a tall, handsome young man, please call me Elizabeth.'

Dressed again, Kenny tries to tidy his hair in front of the mirror over the sink. Now he needs to bend down a little to see himself. Remembers when he'd had to stand on a box. He shuts his eyes, swamped for a moment by memories of a grown-up rubbing his dirty face with a soapy flannel, then turning towards the door, he follows the smell of coffee and goes downstairs to where Gemma is sitting at the kitchen table and Elizabeth is buttering toast. Gemma! Still wearing that beautiful scarf round her neck. Looking so much the same and yet not quite the girl he last saw on her way to school in her brown uniform.

'Kenny, was it you down at the seafront this morning? In the old shelter?'

'Gemma, let the boy sit down and eat before you start badgering him with questions.'

When Kenny sits down opposite Gemma, Elizabeth thinks how bemused he looks. The boy had had that look quite often, years ago. Especially that time when he and Sarah had come for tea and found Donald there in uniform. He clearly hadn't known what to do or say and had turned his face away, hiding it in Sarah's apron. People grow up, but some things stay the same. That's how we can often recognise people we've not seen for years. Small movements of the body, turns of the head, old habits of eyes and mouth.

'It's OK, Elizabeth,' he says. 'Yes, it was, Gemma. I was sleeping.'

Elizabeth has put a plate of bacon, egg and beans in front of him, and a mug of coffee. He wants to talk and he is also longing to eat. He is aware of all the waiting questions in the air, theirs and his. He takes a slurp of coffee. 'I came on a very early train. Spent most of last night dossing in Waterloo Station talking to the pigeons.'

'Eat, Kenny love, don't talk. Gemma, pass the boy the brown sauce. That is, if he still likes it as much as he used to.'

Kenny smiles back at her, but Gemma, as she reaches for the sauce bottle, sees that his hands shake a little as he spreads egg on his toast – immediately feels she wants to help. She always did. Even though he is several months older than her, he'd always seemed in need of her help. She watches him as he finishes the food and hears his sigh as he puts the knife and fork down.

'I went home this morning. Over the road, I mean. Soon as I got here. Our door is red now.' He looks as if he wants to go on, but stops. Leans back into the chair and looks down at the empty plate, eyes watering. Gemma and Elizabeth turn to each other. Neither speak for a moment, but each has the same thought.

'Yes, that red door.' Elizabeth has found her voice. 'Did anyone come out and speak to you, Kenny?'

'A woman came out and she told me Granny had gone. I didn't realise what she meant at first, but she explained.'

'I'm guessing you didn't know, love?'

'No. I didn't know.' His voice is now only a whisper.

Gemma reaches out, takes his hand. 'Kenny, we didn't know where you were,' she says. 'Only somewhere up north. From your postcard. We'd have written, of course, if we'd known.'

'The postcard? Oh, yeah!' Kenny looks down at his hands. 'I wanted to let her know I was all right. Meant to write again, but things got difficult. Complicated. Long story.'

'I wish you had. We couldn't let you know. We wanted to,' Elizabeth says, so quietly, she's not sure Kenny has heard. She pulls out the chair at the end of the table and sits. 'Sarah got quite poorly, with a cough. We kept trying to persuade her to go to the doctor, but she wouldn't, for ages, and then it got worse, of course, and I called an ambulance and went with her to hospital. It was pneumonia.' Kenny is staring but she thinks he's not seeing her. He's trying to picture his grandmother lying in bed in hospital. 'I was with her, Kenny, when she died. She wasn't in pain. They were looking after her well. She was comfortable. And then she just went to sleep.'

Elizabeth gets up again and goes to Kenny and puts her arms round him. He feels her gently kiss the top of his head. Feels Gemma's fingers tighten round his hand.

The long silence doesn't feel uncomfortable. Each has their own image of Sarah, but there is a shared sense of the woman who had been there for so long. Elizabeth knows she has missed her friend and neighbour every day for nearly six months. Gemma has felt Sarah's absence actively since her return from Birmingham just before Christmas. But for Kenny the news of her death is raw and shocking. He is painfully aware of what his unnecessarily long absence may have meant for her. Blaming himself, he is suddenly filled with anger. Anger with Marit. Her fault.

Elizabeth breaks the silence as she pours Kenny another cup of coffee.

'Kenny, it's just an idea but would it help if Gemma took you up to the grave? And you two probably want to talk and catch up a bit more without me sitting on the side-lines. Gemma love, you'll remember where it is, won't you? It's the Highland Road Cemetery, Kenny. Won't take you two long to walk up there.'

He is looking blankly at her for a moment and then gives a quick nod.

'Yes, I'd like that but only if…' He looks across to Gemma.

'Of course, Mum. Kenny, let's do it. But we should go now, if we're going, because they shut at about four this time of year.'

'But leave me your other clothes, Kenny. I'm needing to do a quick wash and I can easily put your stuff in with it. No problem now I have the twin tub. It'll be hanging out on the line by the time you get back.' Kenny feels embarrassed, but goes to get his rucksack from the bathroom and hands it to Elizabeth, hoping she won't take out his shamefully grubby underwear and T-shirt in front of Gemma. Wonders what she'd have thought if she'd seen him on the streets or under the arches by the Thames.

Elizabeth starts to open the rucksack as soon as she hears them shut the front door. She pulls out the underwear, a pair of torn and faded jeans and a black T-shirt with a saxophone emblem on the front. Feeling inside to check if there is more, she feels an unexpected softness and pulls out the pale blue cashmere jumper. Expensive – she says to herself. I wonder who bought him this? And then her searching fingers touch something hard, at the very bottom of the bag. A book. She takes out the stories of Hans Christian Andersen. Faded, pages with torn edges, and on a card inside, "To Kenny, Happy Birthday and Love from Gemma and Elizabeth 1954." She remembers the very cold day that she had helped Gemma choose the book. Her daughter had insisted that her friend would enjoy these stories as much as she did.

The daylight is fading fast in the cemetery as Gemma stands a little apart from Kenny's side, but looking, like him, at the gravestone.

CYRIL GEORGE CRAWLEY

1892–1925

AND HIS BELOVED WIFE SARAH EMILY CRAWLEY

1896–1963

He says, 'Good that she's there. Next to her husband.'

'Yes. It was paid for out of a funeral plan she had with the Co-op.'

'Cyril. She told me about him once. Said he was my grandfather. You wore his hat at the fancy dress at school, remember?'

'Goodness, that's a long time ago. I was a scarecrow and you were a Red Indian chief, weren't you?'

'So…' The questions are bubbling around in Kenny's head, the questions that had been burning away, that had kept him going across Waterloo Bridge and through the long night at the station, and ringing in his head all the way down on the train to Portsmouth, laced with the hope that he'd get answers from the person who knew him best: Granny Sarah – who is in the cold ground in front of him! Who cannot answer any questions anymore! He can't bring himself to ask about his mother, but…

'So, what about my father? Is he here somewhere?'

Gemma can hardly bear to look at him. She thinks, but isn't sure, that there is no answer for Kenny.

'Kenny, we don't know. I mean we don't know who he was. Only the same as she told you…and she told Mum the same… that he drowned in the war when his ship went down.'

'But isn't there anything? A name, a photo, a newspaper announcement?'

'No Kenny, I don't think there is. But when we get back to the house, let's talk with Mum. I'm know she's got a few bits and

203

pieces that were left in your house. It was after the funeral. The agents asked Mum to clear the place before the next tenants got there and…'

'And my mother? Did Granny Sarah ever tell Elizabeth anything? Where she went? Why she never came back?'

'No Kenny, but there is a picture of her. Mum found a photo.'

The light is fading fast, and a cold breeze is whipping around the gravestones, scattering dried dead leaves in swirls along the paths as Gemma suddenly puts her arms round Kenny, who drops his head on her shoulder, and she feels, rather than hears his sob. As she releases him, her scarf slips a little, and Kenny, raising his head to look at her, sees the now faded but still visible markings on her neck where Bruce had grabbed her in his fury.

'Gemma, for God's sake, who did that to you?' Kenny has seen marks like that back on the streets in the worst of times when he was sharing pavements and alleyways with the drinkers and the injectors. Recognises them for what they are. Marks of moments of violence.

Gemma is about to speak, but the sound of a bell being rung interrupts the moment. The cemetery is closing for the night, and they turn towards the gate. Kenny takes one more glance back at his grandmother and his grandfather's grave.

Walking back down Albert Road, past all the junk and antique shops, they realise they are holding hands.

In the kitchen, Kenny's clean clothes are drying on the airing frame above Elizabeth's head as she starts preparing supper. It is mostly Christmas leftovers, but she has some baking potatoes and the last few leaves of a lettuce. She looks down for a moment at the three sets of cutlery and three plates on a tray and a jug of tap water and three glasses. When were there last three people at her table to eat? Her thoughts drift from the present to the past. Donald coming home. Donald drinking beer with his supper. Gemma staring at him as if at a stranger. Which he was to her, of course. And after the years apart, unfamiliar in so many ways to herself. Then in later years, the odd occasions when the couple next door came round for lunch or tea. Ham slices on a plate. Tomatoes in a bowl. Washed lettuce. And sliced peaches with evaporated milk for dessert. And Sarah. Yes, Sarah and Kenny sitting round the kitchen table with her and Gemma. Four of them, comfortable together, the children giggling and talking over each other, nudging at one of their secret jokes. Sarah laying out one of her cakes on a plate. She rarely came empty-handed even though she had so little. When she got ill and frail, Elizabeth found herself reversing the process, taking round soup, stew, or just cups of Bovril when Sarah was not feeling like eating at all. Recently, Elizabeth has mostly eaten quietly on her own, although sometimes has joined Audrey the lodger, who makes her feel so old, (nearly fifty...how did that happen?) But Audrey has a different way of cooking and eating. Spaghetti or rice and strong-smelling sauces, or bright-coloured vegetables stirred together in the same pan, and soup with cheese on toast floating on the top. Elizabeth likes the smell of these exotic dishes but isn't quite sure about them. Of course, she's been offered the odd taste, but it's like Audrey's fancy coffee. Smells wonderful, but the flavour takes some getting used to.

When she hears the front door, she jumps, she's been so deep in her own head.

'Is that you two back? Did you get there in time before it closed?'

'Yes Mum, it's us.' Gemma comes into the kitchen first. 'No messages?' she says with a slight frown.

'No love, nothing. And you found the grave? I was worried you'd get there too late, after the man had rung his bell. It must have been getting on for dark when you got there.' Elizabeth is aware of feeling anxious about the effect on Kenny of seeing Sarah's grave when a day ago he hadn't even known she had died. She knows she is in danger of talking too much. As Kenny comes into the kitchen, he looks up and sees his clean, damp clothing on the airer.

He smiles at Elizabeth. 'Oh, that's great, Elizabeth. Thank you so much.'

As Gemma takes off her coat and the scarf, Elizabeth is surprised and looks across at her daughter, the unspoken question on her face. 'It's OK, Mum. Kenny's seen my bruises, and he knows how I got them. Really, it's alright.'

Kenny says, 'Yes. She's been telling me…not the whole story but…'

'Sit down, Mum. We need to ask you some things. Kenny and I have been talking and we think you can help.'

'Oh, do you?' Elizabeth says, aware of a sliver of anxiety about questions she may not be able to answer. Or won't want to answer. She wants time to think. To be ready. 'Of course, I'll help if I can. But it will have to wait a bit. Right now, I'm starving. And you must be cold and hungry too. Let's get the living room warmed up and get supper first.'

The lamps are switched on, the gas fire lit, and Kenny sits close to Gemma on the settee in the living room. They have eaten the cold chicken and buttered baked potato Elizabeth had insisted they eat before she got the papers out. The tension in the kitchen had made it hard for them to finish the salad. They have left the peaches and evaporated milk to have later.

206

Kenny and Gemma listen in silence to Elizabeth's footsteps above. They know she's gone to fetch the envelope. The one she'd found in Sarah's kitchen drawer.

While they wait, Gemma feels Kenny's eyes on her again. He's looking at the marks on her neck. She'd told him about the final row with Bruce, as they'd walked back along Albert Road, and he in turn had told her a little about his time on the pavements and under the arches in London. How surprisingly easy it was to talk about these dark times, Gemma thought, after not seeing each other for years.

Elizabeth comes in and settles herself in her usual chair and puts the brown envelope on the coffee table between them. The 1945 George the Sixth stamps and Sarah's address seem to stare up at Kenny. When Elizabeth settles her right hand on the envelope, the stamps disappear, and Kenny feels he has lost them. He wants to see them again.

The stamps reappear as Elizabeth takes her hand back, and says, 'Kenny, the things in here are not going to answer all your questions. I don't want you to get your hopes up and then be disappointed, but this is all I have. All I found in Sarah's house.' And she quickly takes everything from the envelope, spreading the pictures, ration books and identity papers out on the table.

Kenny is staring. Gemma thinks he doesn't know what to look at first.

He reaches slowly for the biggest picture and stares at it. It seems familiar to him although he doesn't remember seeing it before. It is the group of people outside the church. The one where someone is holding a baby in a big shawl. Elizabeth points to the baby.

'That's you, Kenny. The baby, all wrapped up in a big shawl, it's you.'

'And is that Granny holding me then?' He's looked up at Elizabeth as he speaks.

'Yes, that's Sarah. Your granny knitted that shawl. Your first blanket.'

Kenny continues to look at the photo for a long moment before pointing hesitantly to the serious-looking young woman who stands awkwardly, arms folded across her waist, hands clutching her elbows. She must have been looking just to the side of the camera lens.

'And her?' Kenny asks.

'That's Yvonne, Kenny,' Elizabeth says quietly. 'Your mum.'

'My mother. That's her? She looks so unhappy. Was she unhappy?'

'Yes, I think she was, although I didn't really know her or Sarah then. I hadn't been in this street very long. But she seemed sad.'

'Was it because of my dad being dead? Or was it because she'd had me?'

The silence in the room seems to hold Kenny's question in the air for a moment. Elizabeth wants to keep breathing, but it feels a struggle. She wants to find the right words for the boy, but what are the right words?

'Kenny, love, Yvonne was very young, and the war was still going on. People were still dying. Disappearing.'

'Like my dad. Gemma says she doesn't know who he was. Don't you know either? Don't you even know his name? Haven't you got even got a photo of him or anything?'

Gemma puts a hand on his.

Elizabeth picks up the photo and turns it over and back again. 'Kenny, we don't know. No idea. Because Yvonne never said. Not even to Sarah, we don't think. You must realise that things were so different then. People were unkind. Said things. When young girls ran into trouble, they were made to feel ashamed. And believe me, things happened that weren't always a girl's fault.'

'So…not something she'd meant to happen? A one-night stand or something? Is that why she went away?'

'I think something like that, yes. It always felt like Sarah knew a bit more, but who knows? So many things got hidden away then. Secrets got kept. Stories got told.'

Kenny slumps into the sofa, looks up at the ceiling, passes a hand over his eyes. Then he sits back up and reaches for the ration book and the identity card. He runs his fingers over the front and back. 'I wonder why she left these behind.' It's not a question he seems to be asking them – more like one he is asking himself. 'I can't remember her at all.' Kenny is struggling to make sense of these facts and guesses and unknowns. He suddenly thinks of Stefan. Stefan, who said he'd looked for missing people. Stefan, who'd talked to him about people going missing in "the fog of war". 'And she went when?'

'You were a couple of months old, as I remember,' says Elizabeth, who wants to make this poor boy feel better. She wants to say something helpful but which will also feel true. She looks up at him. 'But Kenny, I do know that you were loved. Loved absolutely by Sarah and loved by me and loved by Gemma. Isn't that right, Gem?'

Gemma breathes, 'Yes, Kenny,' as she wraps her arms round his shoulders and, as in the cemetery, she feels his heaving sob.

Elizabeth hears the front door shut, and in her mind's eye she follows their disappearing footsteps. It's late. Late for a walk to the seafront, she thinks, but at least the two of them are together. Yet, she wonders, in what way together? They seem to need each other much as they did as children. Now do they need each other differently? To fill a gap, to take the place of someone? But as what? Father, mother, sibling, friend, even lover maybe? And if so, is it for the moment, for a season until the pain goes, or for life? Maybe each of them has a different idea. Do either of them know what the other one needs?

But for now...yes...a walk in the dark, in the cold, to the beach, and maybe Gemma can help Kenny digest the evening's revelations. They'll walk on the beach, listening to the shifting pebbles under their shoes, as she has done so often over the years. Elizabeth imagines, as she continues to sit upright in her chair, that they'll maybe not talk but let the sound of the quiet movement of water soothe their own disturbances. Instead of speaking quietly of their shared memories, they may just hold the pictures in their heads. Of bat-and-ball games in the garden, of racing round the bombsite in their different characters drawn from comics and Saturday morning cinema. Of going off to school hand in hand. For the moment, perhaps that will be enough. It will be what's needed. Gemma will listen to Kenny, even if he isn't speaking. She'll watch for any evidence of his thoughts. She's always been good at that. How often has she come quietly into the kitchen to sit, and after a few moments said something, as if she has heard Elizabeth's unspoken thoughts?

After the contents of the brown envelope had been put back inside, she'd passed it to Kenny. Then she and Gemma had sat quietly as Kenny had tried to smother his sobs by thrusting his arms across his face. Whatever hopes he'd had of finding news of a loving mother, a lost but heroic father, of a brief but loving parental relationship, were all dashed now. She surely couldn't have kept the envelope and its contents in its old place in her chest of drawers and have left the poor boy to a life of endless wondering – to a life of imagining some kind of family, perfect or not, taken from him by war.

Kenny has an arm round Gemma's shoulders. They are sitting close together in the old seaside shelter with collars pulled up to keep the cold sea breeze out. Feeling her shivering, he holds her closer. Gemma rests her head against his chest where she can feel the pace of his breathing. Slower now, quieter. After they'd left the house, while they had been walking towards the shore through the empty streets, she'd heard as well as seen his rapid breathing, cloudy in the cold night air. Her fear was that he could collapse at any moment, could fall apart in front of her like pieces of a broken glass in her hand.

When they'd stopped for a moment in the Rock Gardens and stood next to the old fountain, he seemed to gather himself in some way. 'I'm OK, Gemma. I'm going to be all right,' he'd said, as if reading her mind.

'I know you will be, Kenny.' It was dark but not too dark for them to exchange a small smile. Now, as they sit in the shelter, a car roaring in the distance punctuates their shared silence. 'Kenny, what my mum said…'

'She said a lot.'

'…about you being loved. By us. As well as by Sarah…'

Kenny is staring out into the dark, eyes following the faint lights of a ferry on its way out past the fort that had always seemed to him to just grow out of the sea. How deep must it be there, he thinks. He is imagining being on the boat, standing on deck, water slapping at the hull. On his way somewhere new. Starting again. On his own. Then, with a jolt, he thinks: that's what Yvonne did. Upped sticks and disappeared. And hadn't he done the same, leaving home without saying goodbye? Had sent the one postcard. Which is one more than Yvonne had sent.

When he experiences a sudden surge of anger, Gemma senses the change in his breathing and lifts her head from his chest.

'Kenny? What are you thinking?'

'I only sent one postcard, Gemma. I didn't even let anyone know where I was. Didn't know she'd been poorly. Didn't know she'd died. My own bloody fault. Shouldn't have stayed away so long.'

'Why did you, Kenny? What kept you away for so long? Was it because of that woman in the red car?'

Kenny turns towards her so suddenly she feels unbalanced for a second or two.

'How did you know it was a red car?'

'I saw you at the bus stop that afternoon. I was going to come and speak to you, but just as I waved, this car drew up, and then you were gone in a flash, like magic.'

He has turned away from her and is looking out to sea again. The ferry is fainter now as it slips towards Ryde Harbour.

'Like magic. Yes, it was like magic. Or maybe like I was in a film, or a dream, and it took me too long to wake up. How could I have been so stupid?'

'You and me, Kenny, we both thought dreams could come true, didn't we? That something was going to be good for us – and then it wasn't.'

'Too right! And Bruce? What's going to happen now with you and him?'

'That last evening in Birmingham, when he hurt me properly – not just a shove or a too-tight hold of my wrists – it was like waking up. All the things that I'd half recognised in

212

him, that I'd kept to the back of my mind, came right to the front of my head, if you know what I mean. And I knew he was dangerous and I needed to get out. I was in a panic all the way as I walked into the city. Kept thinking I could hear him chasing me.'

'Gemma, don't you think—?'

'No, Kenny, let me say this. It's important. I knew he didn't love me – just needed me to be there in some way. But now? Now, will he ever let me be? Will he keep away? Every time I hear a car door bang, or footsteps in our street, or hear the phone ring, I panic.'

'The bastard! God, Gemma, that's awful.'

'Awful, yes, but not awful all of the time. When I was a bit down, he'd sense it, and would go out of his way to make me feel special. When I came down here for your granny's funeral, Kenny, I'd had such a wish that you'd be here. All the way down on the train I had that idea. Wondered if you'd be taller. Would you have grown your hair long, like lots of the boys at university? Or have a beard even? But then you weren't there. No one had known where you were or how to get in contact with you. And instead of you, there was Bruce, to fill the gap, kind of thing.'

'I'm so sorry. I should have been there. My fault. I was just – hard to explain now I'm away from her. You see, Marit wanted me there. Didn't want me to – I don't know – didn't want me to be in contact with anyone outside her world. And for a while it was magical, like being in heaven. Feeling so special.'

'And then?'

'Then it started, slowly, slowly, to feel like I was in a spider's web, and each time I had ideas of going somewhere, maybe even home for a visit, she'd pull me back with her spider's sticky threads into her world. Into her bed. Sorry! After a while I just couldn't tell what was real and what was a lie, and I think I started to feel ashamed – until one day I realised, like you did with Bruce, that I was afraid of her. She was an evil puppeteer and I was at the end of her strings. And I had to get away as well. But it's different for me. I just got replaced. Marit won't come after me.'

Kenny is startled as Gemma stands up suddenly, fingers holding tightly to the collar of her coat. 'Let's walk.' And she's already on the move, towards the pier. He's up and soon beside her. 'What's wrong with us, Kenny? What makes it so easy for these people to convince us black is white, that love is... What's the opposite of love? Not hate exactly. More a prison. A place where you get told you are loved, but only as long as you behave in the way that's wanted.' The wind is nearly whipping her words away, but he catches them.

'Do you think if your dad had stayed around, you'd have done things differently?'

'Old Donald? Who knows? I can hardly remember what he looks like, although the smell of beer always reminds me of when he first came back. And you? If Yvonne hadn't left? Or there'd been a father around in your life?'

'A father! My guess, from what Elizabeth was hinting, was that he wasn't around too long. Maybe only enough time to... well, you know! Otherwise, why wouldn't have Yvonne told Sarah who he was? Unless he was married, of course.' When a ship's hooter breaks through the air from the harbour, Kenny turns to Gemma. 'God, that picture of her at my christening – she looked so frozen. Wasn't even looking at me. Didn't want to be there. Probably didn't even enjoy the making of me with whatever his name was. No wonder I went off with Marit and her beautiful smiles. She looked at me properly. Her eyes were amazing. She was extraordinary, you know, and at first... Well, you don't want to know. And then Stefan...'

'That's the guy in London who helped you?'

'Mm. Someone else I left without saying goodbye. He didn't deserve that. He'd been really helpful, really kind. Gave me a place to stay when I had nothing. Fed me. Gave me work. Introduced me to music I'd never heard before, taught me to cook, gave me hope, said I should plan a future, go to college, get qualifications.'

'But you ran away. Why?'

Kenny doesn't answer straight away, as Gemma looks at him, trying to interpret his expression.

'He just forgot himself for a moment.' Kenny is walking faster, getting ahead of Gemma, so she hardly hears him say, 'Sorry, I don't want to talk about it. At least, not now.'

'Can you go back there?'

'Go back? No, how can I? But maybe I might call him sometime. I don't ever want to see or speak to Marit again, but Stefan... God, Gemma, he was crying when I left. I could hear him and he kept saying he was so sorry, while I was packing my bag and walking out of the door.' Kenny has slowed down and they are back together walking side by side.

'You talk about him as if you were fond of him. And he of you?'

'Hmmm. I don't know. Yes. He bought me this blue jumper for a Christmas present. Lent me his old jacket and tie when we went to the jazz club. That was the problem. I think he was fond of me, but maybe not in a way that was comfortable because—'

'Because?' Gemma has stopped under a lamp post and is looking carefully at Kenny's face.

'Because I just liked him. But not like I think he was beginning to like me. Look, I'm fucking freezing. Can we head back now? Elizabeth might be worrying.'

'Yes, let's. It suddenly feels like it's been a very long day.'

They are nearly back to the house when Kenny says, 'What about Bruce? Do you need to write to him to make it clear that it's over?'

'I'm afraid to get in touch with him in any way even by letter.'

'Well don't then. When do you have to go back to Birmingham?'

'In another couple of weeks, I suppose, although I could plead sickness and stay longer. I'll need to find a new place, which won't be easy at this time of year. But otherwise, he'll be back looking for me. God, Kenny! Am I going to have to keep moving on, or will he find another victim?'

'What about the police? He assaulted you, didn't he?'

'Oh, come on, you know how much notice they'd take of that. "A domestic", they'd say. Look, I can't bear to talk about it anymore. And I'm freezing cold, and so are you. Let's go inside and see if we can find some of Mum's magic Ovaltine.'

'Yes. Good idea.' Kenny rests his lips on her forehead.

She smiles up at him and puts both hands to his cheeks before getting out her key and opening the door. Warm air meets them as they step inside.

New Year's Eve

Kenny is out shopping for food. It's the morning of New Year's Eve and he has promised to cook one of Stefan's Italian recipes tonight. He's been sleeping in the little box room since he arrived at the door, exhausted, smelly and in tears, on the day after Boxing Day. There is hardly room for him and his rucksack, let alone to swing a cat, as Elizabeth has said. But he feels at peace. The first night sleeping in the tiny space, listening to the near silence outside, Kenny couldn't quite believe that he was back in his old street. When he'd heard the soft voices from downstairs, of Gemma and Elizabeth getting ready for bed, people who knew him so well when he was a child, he had wanted to cry again. Even after that first very long day he had felt wide awake, lying between sheets and blankets on a set of cushions on the floor, so he'd looked for his book at the bottom of the rucksack and started to read

The Snow Queen but had soon fallen deeply asleep. When he woke in the morning, the book was open and upside down on the floor beside him. As he lay there, remembering what Stefan had said about children's stories, he made up his mind to properly to read the whole book carefully again. He felt sad that in leaving in such a hurry on Boxing Day, he hadn't thought to pick up the books Stefan had given him to read. And again, stretching his arms and legs to the four corners of the room, he had thought of Stefan. Uncomfortable thoughts. Back in London he had started *Brighton Rock* and at first had enjoyed the descriptions of a seaside town not unlike Southsea, but the book quickly got quite intense, reminding him of his own dark and hungry times, the nights when he'd struggled to avoid the kicks, the spit, and other forms of abuse on the pavements of Central London. He had been planning to have a go at *Animal Farm* next, but then he had run away. And now he knew that this was just what his mother had done.

Now Kenny is out searching, with Elizabeth's old string shopping bag and some money, in the familiar streets, for what he needs for the meal. There have been one or two changes in the parade of shops, but it's the same man in the grocer on the corner, although he doesn't seem to recognise him. Kenny buys a packet of ham, some proper long spaghetti in a blue paper wrapper, a tin of tomatoes, and a slab of cheddar. He'd asked if the man had any parmesan cheese but got a blank look. Then at the greengrocer on Albert Road he finds some decent tomatoes, Spanish onions, mushrooms and a bulb of garlic. Wishing for some fresh basil, he's looked but failed to find any, but remembers spotting a jar of some of the dried herb on the lodger Audrey's kitchen shelf, and she won't miss a pinch, although there won't be that sweet aroma of torn leaves that he first experienced in Stefan's kitchen.

He's planning on a rich pasta dish and he hopes he hasn't forgotten any of Stefan's instructions. For a moment he is back in that kitchen, watching the snip-snip of the scissors on the basil leaves and feeling the rub of the wooden spoon on the pan bottom. And that quiet, encouraging voice come into his head, 'That's it, Kenny. Not too much, but more importantly, not too little. Keep stirring.'

Back at the house, Elizabeth has brought out the last of the Christmas pudding from the larder to warm up and have with some custard, and she remembers that there is a bottle of Italian wine in the store cupboard that's been there years, to go with the pasta. She is standing by the cooker with her second cup of tea, when she hears the metallic rattle of the letterbox on the front door. Gemma, still sitting at the kitchen table, freezes, her teacup halfway to her mouth. Elizabeth, turning from the cooker, kettle in hand ready to top up the teapot, looks across at her daughter.

'Gemma, I can't just keep on avoiding the door. It'll be a neighbour or the postman. Just stay there while I go and see.'

'Hello, it's Elizabeth, isn't it?' It is the woman from over the road, from Sarah's old place, and she is holding out a parcel. 'This came to us by mistake, but I think it must be for here. It just says Gemma and the street name. You've got a Gemma here, haven't you?'

'Yes, I certainly have,' Elizabeth says, turning with a smile to reassure her daughter who is now standing, still holding her cup.

'Come in, Mildred, and meet her properly. It's freezing out there. Have a cuppa and sit for a while. Look Gemma, it's something for you, love.'

'Well, don't mind if I do, but must only be a minute. Fred's back there with the little ones, and you know what men are like.' And she makes that kind of a face that some women do when talking about their men. Half pretend-annoyed and half proud. 'And lovely to meet you, Gemma. I've seen you from a distance, of course.'

Elizabeth is quickly reaching for a mug and passing it to Mildred. 'Help yourself to milk and sugar, please. I don't know how you like it yet. One of those things that comes with time when you live in the same place for years.'

'Heavens, so you're one of the long-term residents! I mean, you've been here how long?'

'Oh, forever, since the middle of '44. Gemma was born here, weren't you, love?'

But Gemma is staring at the parcel in her hands. Turning it over, she has seen a sender's address on the back. Petersfield, Sussex. In an unfamiliar hand.

'Then you'd have known the old lady who lived at our little house before us?' Mildred is saying to Elizabeth.

'Well, yes. We knew Sarah very well, and the children went to school together.'

'Oh,' and she hesitates. 'So you must have known the young man who came round just after Christmas.'

'Yes, we—' Elizabeth starts to say, but Mildred is still speaking.

'Lord, I felt dreadful. Somehow, he hadn't heard, you see, about his poor gran. Ran off before I could say anything more. I'd have given him some breakfast, but one minute there, next one gone. And he looked as if he could have done with something inside him.'

'Mildred, don't worry. He came here and he is staying with

us for a while. We hadn't seen him for a long time, but he still feels like family to us. Gemma, isn't that right? Gemma what is it?' Gemma face has frozen. Her white knuckles grip the edge of the table.

'Will you excuse me, Mildred? Sorry, Mum, I just need to— I'll be in my room.'

'Gem, love, what is it?'

But she is already gone.

Upstairs, Gemma sits on her bed and begins to slowly finish unwrapping the parcel. The first covering is of brown paper, sellotaped down. Tearing this off, she sees the Christmas wrapping paper underneath. Stuck to that is an envelope, in that unfamiliar hand again. She opens it to find a small card with a picture of a country church on the front. Inside the card it says, after an address and phone number:

Dear Gemma,

We realise that this will come as a great shock but we need to tell you that Bruce had a tragic accident in his car and was killed. We think he was on his way to see you on Boxing Day with your Christmas present. Bruce told us a lot about you. He was clearly very fond of you and we had been looking forward very much to meeting you at Christmas. We know he would have wanted you to have this.

Of course, we would be touched if you felt able to come to the funeral service.

Regards
Amanda and Gerald Kingston

A cutting from a newspaper falls out.

It is with very great sadness that Mr and Mrs Kingston announce the death of their beloved son, Bruce, on December 26th 1963.

The funeral service will be at St Peter's Church

The Square, Petersfield

On January the 5th at 11.00am

All will be welcome to come to the house after the service

Gemma is sitting very still. She holds the card tightly, but is no longer looking at it. She hears, as if from faraway, Mildred's 'Cheerio'. Hears the door slam. Hears Mildred's heeled shoes crossing over the road, back to her house. Then hears her mother's slippered feet on the stairs.

'Gemma?' Elizabeth half opens the door and takes a tentative look. Then, in seconds, she is there by her daughter's side. Gemma passes her the card and the cutting.

'He's dead, Mum. Bruce. In a car crash. Days ago!'

'Oh Lord in heaven! Come here, love.'

The Christmas parcel lies at their feet, forgotten. The very slight stain and tear from an icy roadside is hardly visible.

Kenny lets himself in the front door with Elizabeth's spare key. Going into the kitchen with his full bag of food, he calls out, 'Hello, I'm back. Anyone for a hot drink and a doughnut?' He'd spotted the sugar-covered doughnuts in the window of the bakers in Albert Road, where he'd gone for a French stick, and had remembered the little bit of money left in his jacket pocket. Now, standing by the kitchen counter, carefully unpacking things, he calls out again, puzzled at the silence. Then he hears Elizabeth's feet on the stairs.

'Kenny, you're back. Yes, tea and a doughnut. What a treat. Lovely.' She is trying to smile, but it doesn't look quite right. She's clearly been crying.

'What's up, Elizabeth? What's happened? You look like you've seen a ghost.'

'No. Well yes. We've had a bit of a shock.'

'What is it? Tell me. Is Gemma OK?' Elizabeth shakes her head, then waves a hand across her face.

'No, she's fine. It's just...' She is standing with a rather dazed look on her face.

'Look, sit down,' he tells her, 'and I'll make you a cuppa.' He picks up the kettle to fill it. Elizabeth puts a hand gently on Kenny's arm before lowering herself into her usual chair.

'It's Bruce. It's about Bruce.'

The kettle bangs onto the counter as Kenny spins around. 'What, here? Has the bastard turned up here?' He is striding towards the door when Elizabeth reaches out and catches at the sleeve of his jacket.

'No! Not here. No, Kenny. No. He's dead.'

'What?'

'He crashed his car. Apparently, he was on his was down here. To see Gemma. She just got a letter from his parents. Then she telephoned them, and that got her in a bit of a state about it. But I think I've calmed her down, and now I hope she's trying to sleep. God, it's dreadful for her, Kenny.'

'When?' Kenny has come back to join Elizabeth at the table. His exciting supper supplies sit forgotten on the counter.

'Boxing Day, but in the dark, very early – there was ice. On the A3 somewhere. This side of Butser Hill I think.'

Boxing Day. While he was asleep in his bed at Stefan's. Kenny passes a hand over his face as he tries to put these pictures together.

'And Gemma? Should I go up and—'

'No, best leave her for a bit longer, Kenny. It's been a huge shock.' Kenny reaches out to put a hand on hers.

Kenny gets up to finish filling the kettle and puts it on the gas. It strikes him that now he's being the comforting grown-up to this woman who had put her arms round his small body so often, to comfort him, all those years ago. He reaches for a mug, choosing the blue and white one he's noticed she often uses. They sit in silence for a while.

'But, you know,' Elizabeth says quietly, 'I wonder if, after a while, it will be a relief. I know that sounds a terrible thing to think. Don't, for goodness sake, tell Gem I said it. But you must have noticed how jumpy she's been. Anyone knocking at the door, the phone ringing, cars driving past. Bruce hurt her, and he scared her badly and I could have throttled him myself—'

'Do you think she was afraid he'd never leave her in peace?'

'God, yes, Kenny. I am ashamed to say it, of course,' she says, lifting her face to look at him, 'but if I'm honest, I can't say I'm not glad. For Gemma's sake. But of course, the poor parents. Strange though. Gemma said that when she spoke to them, they sounded, not tearful, almost cold, and rather matter of fact. Didn't ask her anything, except why she'd not come with him for Christmas. They want her to go to the funeral, and she doesn't know if she can bear to. What do you think?'

'Why? Has she ever met them before? And do they know what a bully their son is? I mean was? How could she go to a funeral and pretend?'

The sound of the kettle boiling leaves the question hanging, unanswered. When Kenny has filled the pot, he takes two doughnuts out of the paper bag on the counter and puts them on a plate in front of Elizabeth. After he's poured them each their tea, she reaches for one.

'Aren't human beings extraordinary. We can eat a cake and drink tea in spite of—'

'Hot sweet tea is good for shock.'

'Reminds me of the war. Friends who worked nights at the first-aid post used to talk about making sweet tea for people coming in from the raids. Made the world feel less terrifying.'

'Mum?'

They hadn't heard Gemma on the stairs. She is by the door, barefoot and wearing an old, baggy cardigan, wrapped like a blanket, over a nightdress.

'Gemma love, come and sit. Look, tea and doughnuts from Kenny.'

Gemma is still in the doorway.

'Mum, have you told him?'

'Yes,' says Kenny, and in a moment, he is by her side to put his arms round her and guide her to a chair.

'Kenny, they said… They said they were expecting me to come with him for Christmas,' Gemma says, as she sinks into the chair. 'I told Mum, they thought we were getting engaged. They actually sounded cross with me.'

'They'll be in shock, Gem. Take no notice. Anyway, you weren't engaged, were you? Where the hell did they get that idea?'

'She, his mother, said he'd written to them a few weeks ago.' Gemma is standing up again, holding the old cardigan tightly across her chest. 'He'd told them he was going to propose on Christmas Day. But I'd never said I'd go there. He knew I was coming here, I kept telling him on the phone, I said Mum needed me here for Christmas, especially after Sarah not being here anymore. So that last night in Birmingham, when he arrived out of the blue, I couldn't understand why he was so insistent, getting angrier and angrier. Didn't want to take no for an answer, and that's…that's when he hurt me.'

Outside in the garden it is dark. Kenny has been standing there for a while, listening to the distant sound of cars, the occasional shouts of people on their way to a party, a single firework in the distance as it scatters its scraps of light, the very slight rustle of almost bare trees. He's not sure what he's been thinking. Just felt he needed a few minutes alone, with his tumbling feelings. The light from the kitchen shines through the window. He smiles to himself, catching the memory of the Christmas lantern he'd made in the infants' school with coloured tissue pieces and thick black paper. Back in the warm kitchen, he smells the mix of garlic and tomatoes, onions and ham. Going back to the stove, he stirs and then tastes his sauce with a spoon, before adding a few small pinches of black pepper and salt. He can hear the bathwater running upstairs where Elizabeth has persuaded Gemma to have a long soak while he cooks supper. Elizabeth has found some bath salts that a friend gave her for Christmas and the lavender smell is already drifting down the stairs to mingle with the aromas from Kenny's sauce. The whole business of cooking like this is keeping Stefan to the front of Kenny's mind, and he can almost hear his voice. 'Not too much, dear boy, but definitely not too little. Taste and taste again as you go along.' He still hasn't telephoned him. Maybe he will tomorrow. Anyway, Stefan will probably be out with friends tonight. New Year's Eve, after all. He will be listening to jazz at his club, or eating and drinking at Jimmy's or the Amalfi. Or maybe he'll be cooking something wonderful for his friends, ossobuco, or saltimbocca. Or one of those French stews that you have to cook for hours. He'd promised Kenny that he'd teach him how—

'Look, I've found some red candles for the table.'

Elizabeth is there in the kitchen and he's been so far away, back in the London flat, that he didn't hear her come back downstairs.

'I got them for me and Gemma for Christmas Day, and would you believe? We forgot to put them on the table. Kenny? You were miles away.'

He puts his tasting spoon down and leans back on the counter, looking down at the floor.

'You look as if you need to talk,' she says firmly. 'So, tell me. Let's talk now, While Gemma is in the bath.'

He shrugs his shoulders, still looking down.

'You've had so much to think about in just a few days, haven't you?'

He's still staring down at the lino.

'Hard to know where to start.' His voice is so quiet, she can hardly hear him. 'And I don't want to spoil the sauce.' He looks up with an attempt at a smile.

'It smells wonderful, and I can't tell you how comforting it is to have someone cooking for us. And Kenny, it's so good for us to have you here in the house right now.'

'You're right. There's been too much to think about. Granny being dead for months and I never knew. The grave. All those things you showed me, the photos, my mother, the ration book. Then the thing with Gemma being hurt and then today…about Bruce. I keep thinking stupid things like what if he hadn't crashed – what if he had turned up here? What if he'd sweet-talked her again?'

'Do you think I'd have let him in?'

'Don't know. Would you?'

Elizabeth goes over to the stove and turns the gas off under his sauce. She pulls out a chair from the table to sit nearer to him. 'I first saw Bruce when he lived round here when they first met. You know he came to your grandmother's funeral and they got chatting afterwards. I thought he seemed nice enough, quite polite to me, for a student, and clearly keen on Gemma. But listening to her… When she told me how he'd been, well, I told her, I've met his type before. Cinderella's Prince Charming turns into Bluebeard. It's not a new story.'

Kenny looks up again. 'That's funny!' he says, but he isn't smiling.

'What is?

'It's like something Stefan said. About children's stories always being about something true. That's why those stories have lasted so long, he said. And now I'm thinking Bruce started out as Prince Charming and then suddenly—' He puts his hand over his eyes.

Elizabeth has noticed how often he does that. She remembers him as a small boy, turning into his grandmother's apron to shut out something difficult to understand. But now that there's no Granny and no apron, he has to use his hand.

'Then he turns into a monster, an ogre,' she says, 'and tries to keep his Beauty inside his castle.'

'Like me and Marit. I was in her magic castle.'

'And then you wanted to leave.' Kenny nods, hand over his eyes again. Sighs.

'She was so extraordinary. She made me feel like a prince!' He turns to the counter and bangs his fist. 'Then she turned into some kind of a witch! Or a spider.'

Elizabeth is thinking, as she stands and begins to lay the table with clean cutlery, that Kenny and Gemma have more in common than their childhoods.

'A spider?' she asks.

'Yes, a spider, because she lured me. She was beautiful, she had ways of making me feel so good, but it was all like a spider's sticky threads. And then when she'd caught me, she started to devour me.'

Elizabeth nods. 'Yes, that's what they do. A good way to put it, Kenny, love.' They look at each other for a long moment. Elizabeth takes a big breath and stands up. 'But now, the smells from your cooking pot are making me realise that I want to have a glass of wine. To drink to you and Gemma escaping from your spiders and Bluebeards and to you both being here. Kenny, the wine is in that cupboard next to the sink, and the corkscrew is in the drawer.' As she turns away from him to reach for the glasses in the small wall cupboard, Kenny doesn't see the fingers that go quickly to wipe her eyes. She sets the glasses on the table and goes to relight the gas under the sauce. 'I think you might need a bit of water in this, what do you think? I know you were planning for us to be eating sooner. Do you want me to put the water on to boil for the spaghetti yet? I hope Gemma will be down soon.'

'OK.' Kenny has opened the wine and pours two glasses. 'Yes, I think so. Stefan always says—' Kenny stops and takes a sip of his wine.

'Kenny, love, do you have his number?'

'Stefan's? No. Well, yes, I suppose it's in my head.' Kenny looks up at her, surprised. 'Why?'

'It is New Year's Eve. Don't you want to phone him? You're thinking about him, obviously, and maybe he's thinking about you.'

'Yes. I know. I should try. But he'll probably be out. He has lots of friends.'

'Or maybe he'll be home. And he may be worrying about you. So why don't you try?'

It is getting on for midnight. The wax from the red candles has pooled on the table top. The three pudding plates are scraped clean. The bottle of wine is three quarters empty. Elizabeth reaches across Kenny's empty chair to her daughter.

'Gemma, love, you OK?'

'Mum, I'm fine. You were right. I did need to speak to them. But no. I'm not going to the funeral. Really, it would be too awful. I'd have to pretend…them thinking we were practically engaged, when…you know. Goodness knows what he was thinking of, saying all that to them about us getting married.'

Elizabeth nods. They can hear Kenny's voice, and they are both looking towards the door into the hall where the telephone lives. Although they can't hear what he is saying, they look back at each other and smile.

'Sounds like he's found someone in,' says Elizabeth.

'Good. He needs to be able to say sorry to that man.'

'Yes, and to say thank you. If Stefan hadn't come to Kenny's rescue, he wouldn't be here with us now, would he?' They look towards the door again.

'No, he'd be sleeping out on the streets still. And then we'd have had to cook our own New Year's Eve supper! Mum, that food he cooked was lovely, wasn't it?'

When the door opens, and Kenny comes back in, he is smiling.

'Stefan says I must say hello to you both from him.' Gemma looks up at him and claps.

'Well done, Kenny,' Elizabeth says.

'And I told him what I cooked tonight and he said it was a pity I couldn't find fresh basil, but maybe it was a sign I should get on a proper cookery course somewhere. He's going to find out about where is good, and how I could get a grant. I said sorry for running away and…and he said sorry for…you know…his mistake.'

'So, it was the right thing to do, to phone him, wasn't it, Kenny? But look, it's gone five to twelve. Let's pour this last bit of wine into our glasses before midnight. Then, I hope you both remember the New Year's Eve tradition?'

'Of course, Mum,' Gemma says, and laughing, they each take their glass of wine and head for the front door, grabbing coats on the way through the hall. They get outside just as all the church bells start chiming, and before this sound has died away, the glorious noise of the hooters from the collection of ships in the harbour blasts into the air to be heard all over the city.

'Happy New Year,' says Elizabeth, putting her arms round both of them. 'Time to make a resolution and a wish.'

And there they stand till the noise dies away and the quiet and cold catches Elizabeth's attention. 'Come on, you two,' she says, as she heads inside. 'Ovaltine time.'

'Gemma?' Kenny is still looking up at the sky.

'What, Kenny? Now don't you dare tell me your wish. That's bad luck.' She smiles up at him.

'No, it's just – I think I need to go back to London and see Stefan. After speaking to him tonight, you know…'

'Yes, Kenny, you should. He's been good to you.'

'I know you've got to get back to Birmingham, but if I stay up there, in London, do you think you might write to me sometime? Or can I call you?'

'You never know, Kenny, I might even come and visit you,' she mumbles as her head drops to rest on his chest.

Looking down at the top of her head Kenny hears, and smiles.

Acknowledgements

Huge thanks to my sister, Maureen Armstrong for her patience, encouragement and good sense. And to Roger for being there on Zoom during lockdown.

Gratitude to the many dear friends, in no particular order, who have generously read and responded to chapters as I have been writing: Jenny Dover, Sally Penrose, Greta Sadur, Maggie O'Hagan, Anne Casimir , Paul Bennett , Lynette and Maurice Oliphant , Olwen and David Anderson , Andy Tudor, Heather Geddes , Barbara Rowlands, Peter Westland, David Winn and John Morton; to the lovely co -writers I met at City University for their continued support; to Adriana in Portugal for her annual Moonluza Seminars on Fairy Stories at Sintra which left Hans Christian Andersen's Snow Queen so much in my mind, inspiring this project. And to all at SilverWood Books for helping a project become a book.

Gillian Fernandez Morton